He waited until she glanced up. The wary darkness had vanished somewhat, but not totally. "You okay being here?" he asked.

"I see the shooting when I close my eyes. It hardly matters if I'm here or back at the house."

Not that he could blame her. The latest shoot-out was on a slow-motion reel in his head, as well. "For a few hours last evening you seemed to forget."

She slipped her fingers through his. "And I plan to use that tactic again tonight."

"Never been called a tactic before." This woman could call him anything she wanted. Could do anything she wanted with him. They'd been on fast-forward since they met, and he did not want to slow them down.

Still, hand-holding at a crime scene qualified as unprofessional and borderline stupid, so Ben gave the back of her hand a quick rub then let go.

Even though every bone in his body begged him not to.

RELENTLESS

—

HelenKay Dimon

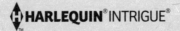

Recycling programs
for this product may
not exist in your area.

To Laura Bradford and Dana Hamilton—
I'm thrilled to be working with both of you.

ISBN-13: 978-0-373-74809-9

RELENTLESS

Copyright © 2014 by HelenKay Dimon

Printed in U.S.A.

ABOUT THE AUTHOR

Award-winning author HelenKay Dimon spent twelve years in the most unromantic career ever—divorce lawyer. After dedicating all that effort to helping people terminate relationships, she is thrilled to deal in happy endings and write romance novels for a living. Now her days are filled with gardening, writing, reading and spending time with her family in and around San Diego. HelenKay loves hearing from readers, so stop by her website, www.helenkaydimon.com, and say hello.

Books by HelenKay Dimon

CAST OF CHARACTERS

Ben Tanner—A former NCIS special agent and current member of the Corcoran Team. He doesn't hide his interest in the pretty nurse from his last job. When she says no to a date, he keeps asking until he gets a yes. All goes well until she's attacked after they say goodnight, making him wonder if he's the true target or if she is.

Jocelyn Raine—She fought off a stalker and put that life behind her. After relocating and starting over as a nurse in a different state and at another hospital, she is ready for a quiet life. A normal, scare-free one. Then Ben, with his guns and his undercover work, walks into her life, and nothing is ever the same.

Gary Taub—He possesses the money, resources and power to make things happen. He also has a new obsession with Jocelyn and a taste for revenge—a potentially dangerous combination. Only he knows how far he will go and if he can do it alone.

Colin Grange—He's Taub's right-hand man. He's seen the boss's plans, but is there more to him than the boss thinks?

Glen Willoughby—The detective shows up everywhere and isn't afraid to issue a few threats against the Corcoran Team. He insists on being involved in all aspects of the investigation, which makes more than one team member wonder which side he's on.

Kent Beane—He's a simple banker...or is he?

Ed Ebersole—He's bank security and went missing when the danger came. He's helping now but the Corcoran Team is still watching and waiting to see what he'll do next.

Connor Bowen—The leader of the Corcoran Team is wrestling with some heavy-duty secrets of his own. He remains focused and determined, but whatever is on his mind is starting to affect the team.

Chapter One

Jocelyn Raine walked under the wrought-iron archway and followed the path to her garden apartment. It was just after nine and the sun had disappeared behind the Annapolis, Maryland, horizon about a half hour ago. Lights inset in the pavers crisscrossed, highlighting the way as she turned right and jogged up the three steps to her front door.

Her cell buzzed at the same time she reached for her keys. While juggling her small purse, she almost dropped the phone. It slipped out of one hand but she caught it in the other before it hit the hard concrete of the small porch.

She swiped her finger over the screen. The promised check-in text from Ben Tanner greeted her. The guy had light brown hair in a short, almost military cut and the most compelling olive-green eyes she'd ever seen.

She could describe the color exactly because she'd stared into them all night across the dinner table on their first date. Add in the linebacker shoulders and that scruffy thing happening around his chin, and no sane woman could brush him off without a second look.

It all worked…except for the part where he carried a gun. She hated guns. She wasn't a fan of violence and despised being scared. She hadn't seen a horror movie since she was a teen. All of which explained why the guy had to ask six times before she finally agreed to go out with him tonight.

Didn't help that within the first two days of knowing Ben, she'd watched him run, shoot, dive, guard and wrestle a scary dude to the ground. All in the critical-care unit of the hospital where she worked, and all while sporting an injury. He'd been shot in the upper arm but that hadn't stopped him from setting up next to a guy in a coma, insisting the unconscious man needed a guard.

And that was why she had finally said yes to him. Something about the former NCIS special agent broke through her defenses. Just a few minutes ago he had insisted, in that respectful voice, that he walk her to the door. She had said no to avoid the awkward "to kiss or not to kiss" confusion, though he was a temptation.

She texted back that all was well and slipped her keys into the locks, first the dead bolt and then the standard one. A woman couldn't be too careful. She'd learned that the hard way.

Once inside, the three-inch pumps came off first. She sighed in relief when her feet hit the thick area rug. That would teach her to wear sexy shoes. Ben only saw them for a second anyway before she tucked them under the table, so she didn't get the point.

The light next to the couch bathed the open area in a soft glow. After resetting the lock and dumping everything but the cell on the table just inside the door, she headed for the family-room area to her right. Ben could text again, so why not be ready?

She looked around for the remote. The television provided background noise, but she had to turn it on first. Ducking, she checked the floor, then the couch cushions. Spinning in a circle, she scanned the room. She always kept it in the basket on the center of her square coffee table. Her gaze went back to that spot, but it still wasn't there.

An odd chill moved across the back of her neck. She blamed the air conditioner she'd set lower than normal to battle the unusual June heat. But then her gaze came to rest on the magazines spread over the coffee table. She stacked them in a pile. Every day and always.

Some people called her obsessive-compulsive, or OCD. She preferred the term *overly neat*.

Either way, she put stuff in its place, and things were not the way she had left them two hours ago.

All thoughts of her sexy date fled.

The chill morphed into a warning itch. She'd been in this situation before and this time she didn't ignore the alarm bells. With a quick look at her phone, she clicked on Ben's name and waited for it to ring on his end. The reaction might be overblown but—

She sensed movement. A change in the air in the room. Little things, almost imperceptible things. A heat—a presence—right behind her.

She spun around as her hand dropped and something brushed against her cheek. A sweet smell hit her dead-on and she shook her head to evade the pungent scent.

A scream died in her throat when a knife waved in front of her. She looked from the muscled arm to the face hardened by lines around the eyes and mouth. A man, tall, bald and dressed completely in black.

Light bounced off the blade. Her breath hitched in her chest as fear hammered through her, threatening to knock her down.

She glanced at the white cloth in his fist. The lingering smell triggered a memory. Nursing school…chloroform. They no longer used it as an anesthesia in hospitals, but she had read about it in medical-history class and had a lab tech describe it in depth during a tour.

She knew through every quaking cell in her body what this man intended to use it for. She vowed right there not to leave this apartment with him, and that meant staying conscious.

"Who are you?" she asked.

"Don't make this difficult," he said in a harsh whisper. Every muscle in her body tensed. Her palm ached. She forgot about the phone until she looked down and saw her death grip on it.

The attacker knocked the cell to the floor and stepped toward her, filling the last bit of safe distance between them. The hand with the cloth went to her throat. His fingers squeezed and her breath was cut off.

She clawed and punched at his hands, walloping him with both fists while she turned her head away from the heady scent assailing her nose and throat. She kicked out but one forceful hit against his shin caused pain to vibrate from her bare foot up her back.

He didn't even flinch.

Just as she lifted her knee to slam into his groin, the knife flashed in front of her eyes again. The flat line of his mouth inched up on one side. The smile was sick, feral, and her stomach churned in terror.

He held the blade close to her eye. "Where is it?"

"What?"

"No games. I want it now."

She fought through the waves of panic shaking through her and tried to process the question. It didn't make sense. "I don't know—"

With a flick of his wrist, he shook her as if she were a rag doll. "Lying won't save you."

The back of her legs banged against the chair behind her. She rose on tiptoes to keep from losing touch with the ground. He had to be over six feet, and at five-five she didn't have the strength or the height to take him on.

"You have the wrong person." The words scratched against her dry throat and her fingers wrapped around his, trying to ease the punishing hold.

"I guess you want to do this the hard way. We'll see how sorry you are after a few hours of convincing." He threaded the end of the knife through her hair. "I am very good at my work."

His hollow laugh sent tremors running through her. The rush of blood to her head made her dizzy. But she had to stay on her feet. Had to think.

"Tell me what you want."

"Tsk, tsk, tsk." He waved the knife back and forth in front of her nose in time with the annoying noise. "Don't play dumb."

"Please." Begging, running—even with her energy reserves low she would try anything.

"You are done causing problems." He scraped the knife's tip over her skin.

She flinched and felt a prick. If there was pain, it didn't register. Not with the adrenaline coursing inside her.

But he just stood there, staring at her. Her fingers went numb from the desperate clenching around his arm. Her heart thudded hard enough to echo in her brain.

Lying. She went with lying. Her breathy voice barely rose above a choked whisper. "I'll tell you what you want."

"That's a good girl."

She pretended to cough. Let the rasp in her voice back up her lie. "Can't breathe."

As if she weighed nothing, he threw her into the chair. Her back slapped against the cushion and she gripped the armrests to keep from slipping down on the material.

The plan was to spring up and out of the seat again, screaming and flying at him as she attacked. Nails, feet, hands, she'd use them all and bring the lamp with her as a weapon.

As soon as she moved, he clamped a hand over her wrist. Trapped it against the chair and pressed down. Put his weight into it. The intense pressure had her crying out.

The knife flashed again. "Not one sound or I break it."

His head turned toward the door. One minute he was in front of her. The next she was up and he stood behind her with the knife touching her throat. "Sounds like we have company."

BEN SMILED WHEN he saw her number light up his phone. Putting the car back in Park, he let the engine idle as he stopped in the middle of her apartment complex's parking lot. "Change your mind about letting me come in?"

Silence greeted him. No, not silence. Shuffling and footsteps. And something that sounded like a muffled shout.

Everything inside him stilled as he strained to hear. All his years of training came roaring back, from the navy to NCIS to his current position with the Corcoran Team. He beat back the urge to race in, gun firing. He needed to know what was happening, if anything even was. And the nerve pulsing by his temple suggested it was.

More moving and a loud crinkling sound as if the phone was breaking in two. After a few seconds her voice boomed through the confusing thuds.

Who are you?

Ben didn't bother to turn off the car. Reaching over the center console, he pressed his index finger in the lock reader, and the compartment next to his radio popped open. With a gun in his hand, he got out.

One in his hand. The other at his ankle. That should do it.

Without looking down, he hit a series of numbers on his cell and lifted it to his ear. After two rings, the line clicked and he started talking. "Apartment six. Now."

Without hanging up, he slipped the cell in the front pocket of his black pants. That would be enough. His teammate Joel Kidd would track the phone, and someone, or a whole group of them, would come blazing in. Until then, it fell to him to assess and rescue.

Crouched and running, he slipped down the pathway that ran through the center, stopping one apartment down. Constantly scanning the area, he looked for trouble. Except for the muffled voices from a television and the wail of a child a few doors up, everything stayed quiet in the comfortable suburban area.

Her door and the drapes to her front window were closed. He could see the light on inside. Everything seemed normal. He knew that wasn't true. And if he'd misread the scene, he'd apologize after. No way was he asking for permission or explanations first.

With a long exhale, he controlled his breathing, forced concern for Jocelyn out of his mind and put on the back burner the memory of how skittish she was to even go on a date. She would be okay. He would make sure of that.

Keeping his steps as silent as possible, he bounded up the stairs. He picked up the low murmur of a male voice. With a light touch, he checked the knob. He had the element of surprise on his side and tried to plan the best way to use it.

Then he heard her scream, and all common sense vanished.

Raising a leg, he nailed his heel into the door right by the knob. The wood split and the lock broke. There was a huge crack as the door slammed open and a hinge snapped.

Somewhere in the distance, a dog barked but Ben ignored it. All of his focus centered on Jocelyn and the man pulling her out of the chair and wrapping an arm around her neck while he hid behind her like a trapped rat.

Ben took in the knife and did a quick glance around the room for a potential partner to this guy. Then he stared at her. The attacker had her long auburn hair pinned under his arm. His hold hiked up her skirt high on her thighs. Nothing torn or ripped. The disheveled state suggested she was thrown around but that the attack hadn't gotten as far as this guy planned.

Those huge blue eyes pleaded with Ben and

her hands shook where she grabbed on to her attacker's arm. She wasn't crying or screaming. She stayed stiff and maintained eye contact.

Good woman.

Gun up, Ben moved into the room and kicked the pieces of what remained of the door shut behind him. Having an innocent neighbor wander by would only cause more trouble. Kids and families lived in this part of town. Someone might interfere. That meant the death toll could rise in a second.

Ben ran a quick mental inventory. The other man's face didn't look familiar. He held a knife, not a gun, though he could have more weapons handy. Clear eyes and dark clothes perfect for a silent attack.

Yeah, this wasn't a junkie looking to steal jewelry. Possibly a professional, though that didn't make sense. Jocelyn was a nurse, not a field agent.

Something else was going on here. Ben would figure out the "what" later. Once the man no longer touched her.

"Step away from her," Ben said with his voice as steady as the hand holding the weapon.

The man's eyes narrowed but his arm tightened against her throat. "Who are you?"

Confusion and maybe a touch of worry. Ben

knew he could use those to his advantage. "Put the knife down."

"You don't seem to understand who's in charge."

"I am." But Ben needed that blade away from her skin. She already had a nick where a small trickle of blood welled.

"You shoot me, you shoot her."

The man underestimated his opponent. Also a good sign in Ben's view. Bravado had taken down more than one otherwise strong man. "Actually, no."

The attacker ran his nose over her hair and the side of her face. The inhale was deep and exaggerated. "She is lovely."

Ben didn't say a word. Didn't so much as twitch. One sign of weakness and Jocelyn could get stabbed or worse.

The man pointed the end of the knife at Ben. "Is she yours?"

There wasn't a good answer, not one that would help her, so Ben continued to stay quiet.

"Ben." Her soft voice carried a wobble.

The attacker smiled in a way that promised pain. "Sounds as if the pretty lady knows you."

When Ben didn't respond, the man's mouth flattened and twisted into a look of pure hate. "Gun on the floor now or I will carve her into tiny pieces."

Her chest heaved and a strangled sound escaped her throat.

Ben watched the light fade from her eyes and knew it was time to act. "Okay, enough."

His gaze locked on hers. With a subtle bounce, he glanced down at her arm. Then he did it again. The heavy breathing forcing her chest up and down in rapid movements slowed and she frowned. He hoped she got the hint.

"Do it now." The attacker barked out the order.

Putting his hands in the air, Ben held up his gun. "Let's stay calm."

The attacker waved the knife around, getting far too close to her face. "Stop stalling."

"My arms are going down." Ben hoped that last attempt delivered the message to Jocelyn.

He had only seconds and a minimal window for error. With his knees bent, he lowered his body and hands toward the floor. The attacker scowled but his focus centered on Ben, right where Ben wanted it.

He set the weapon on the carpet and watched the other man shift his weight. Right when the tension eased, Ben put his palm near his foot, pretending to push up again.

"Now!" he shouted.

In one smooth move, he came up. His second gun slid out of its holder and arced through the air right as Jocelyn smashed an elbow into her attacker's stomach.

"Humph." The man bent over. When he came up again, he roared with a sound of fury that bounced off the walls.

Ben's bullet struck the man's forehead and cut off the sound.

Jocelyn was tight up against Ben with her arms wrapped around his neck before the other guy hit the floor. Ben looked over her head. The bullet hole and trail of blood told him the attacker was dead. So did the look of horror frozen on his silent face.

Still, Ben didn't take any chances. Pushing Jocelyn behind him, he stepped over the attacker's legs and kicked the knife away. After a quick pulse check, Ben's heart finally stopped thundering.

"Is he dead?" Her voice shook.

When Ben turned around, he saw every one of her muscles quaking. Those eyes were wide enough to swallow her entire face. But she was on her feet and not curled up in the corner. She'd given him the assist without any training or lengthy explanation.

Man, he was impressed. "You did great."

"I think I'm going to throw up."

Okay, not his favorite response. "You're probably entitled to, but I kind of wish you wouldn't."

"Looks like I'm too late." Wearing jeans old enough to be faded near white and a dark beard from days without shaving, Joel stepped in the doorway.

Before Ben could make the introductions, Jocelyn bent down and grabbed the other gun. As she aimed it at Joel, the barrel bobbled from the trembling of her arm. "I will shoot you."

Joel's eyes widened and his hands went into the air. "Hold on there."

"Whoa, Jocelyn." Ben reached around her and lowered her arm with the softest touch he could manage in a crisis. "This is Joel Kidd—he's with me."

She glanced at Ben over her shoulder and a haze fell over her eyes. "Joel?"

She should recognize the name from the assignment Ben had been on when he met her. Joel never came to the hospital but Ben had mentioned him. He had talked about him again tonight when he spoke about a friend with a car fetish.

Joel flashed her a smile. "Ma'am."

If she was impressed with Joel and what most women seemed to find irresistible in him, she didn't show it. She spun around to face Ben again. All the color had drained from her face. "What is going on?"

That was exactly what he planned to find out.

Chapter Two

There were more than eight men in her apartment. Jocelyn couldn't give an exact number because she stopped counting when Ben's friends—he called them his team—arrived and the police showed up. Even a stray neighbor or two poked their heads in before being pushed behind the crime-scene tape.

Officers shifted in and out of her family room. A few took notes and circled every piece of anything left on the floor post-attack. They'd snapped photos and a Detective Willoughby asked her questions until her mind went blank.

Now they trampled over every inch of her floor as Ben talked with them, pointing from the door to the couch and explaining things she couldn't hear. They must have mattered to him because he kept up a steady stream of talking while two uniformed officers listened and nodded now and then.

Ever since Ben escorted her out of the fray

and to the barstool in her kitchen, she hadn't moved. She didn't think she *could* move. Her bare feet balanced on the bottom rung, frozen despite the humid night. Ben had put a sweater over her shoulders but she couldn't feel the material against her skin.

The sirens had stopped wailing but the rumble of conversations continued all around her. She heard a clatter and creaks and looked up to see a crew in blue jackets file in with a gurney. There were evidence bags and a huge red stain under the head of the unknown man sprawled on her floor.

Something inside her brain started circling, around and around, and she almost fell over.

"Hey." Ben stepped in front of her, blocking her view of the chaos and holding her steady with hands on her forearms. "You okay?"

If anyone but him, any voice but that soft, reassuring tone, had asked the question, she might have lost it. The calm demeanor only held so long. With the adrenaline rush gone and the shock of what could have happened settling in, her mask slipped. She felt raw, as if someone had flipped her inside out.

She managed a half smile. It was forced, but she tried. "Do you want an honest answer?"

"Probably not." A policeman tapped Ben on the shoulder and he waved the officer away.

Suddenly desperate, she grabbed Ben's hand

and pulled him back to face her. Through everything, he kept her centered. Focused.

His arrival had given her hope. He had sent her the signal when he needed her to fight off her attacker. Then he had saved her with a single shot.

For a woman who had seen so much pain and death on the job, it was the terror she'd experienced in her home this second time that threatened to break her apart. Smash her right into pieces on the floor.

After all those months of learning to handle her anxiety and dealing with the newfound issues of needing everything just so, she was plunged back into a cycle of spiraling fear.

But he, a guy trained to kill, the exact type she should have run from, had proved to be a lifeline. She searched her mind for the right words. When nothing came to her, she went with something heartfelt but simple.

"Thank you," she said as she squeezed his hand.

He leaned in as those intense eyes softened. "You saved yourself. You called and left the line open, which let me know you were in danger. You nailed him in the stomach when I needed the distraction to get the upper hand."

"I got lucky."

"No, you used your head." Ben warmed her hand in both of his with a gentle rubbing. "Without your fast thinking, this would have turned out differently."

"So, the urge to heave up my dinner will pass?"

He chuckled, rich and as soothing as a sweet caress. "Eventually."

A tall man with black hair and startling bright blue eyes walked over. He wore khakis and a polo shirt. Not a police officer but definitely in charge. Everyone certainly acted as if he was. He also looked familiar. Jocelyn knew the face, but the waves of exhaustion crashing over her now made finding the memory impossible.

He spared her a quick glance before launching into conversation. "You're going to need to do an inventory, but nothing obvious is missing."

Ben dropped her hand but rested his palm on her shoulder. "Jocelyn, do you remember Connor Bowen?"

Relief battled with the need to close her eyes as she leaned against Ben. The pieces from the past few months fell together—the hospital and the coma patient. Endless rounds of questions about when the man would wake up and how quickly the nurses could clear the floor if needed. "He's your boss."

Connor held out his hand and gave hers a shake. "That's how I like to think of it."

"No overturned drawers. Electronics are all here. I saw some jewelry." Another man walked up, reading from a list and ticking off each item. "The bedroom is painfully neat."

Yeah, that described her. Painfully neat. She decided to remind the guy she was sitting right there before he said anything embarrassing about how her underwear sat in stacks arranged by color. "Hello."

Ben pointed at the newcomer. "And this is Davis Weeks. He's basically the second in command at the Corcoran Team."

She remembered the company name. Sort of.

"Ma'am." Davis nodded, then launched right back into the rest of his speech. "There's no identification on the guy. There's a chloroform-soaked rag on the floor, so he came prepared and likely didn't expect a fight."

A bone-crushing tremor shook through her. "He tried that first, then went with the knife."

Ben swore under his breath. "The important thing is he didn't hurt you."

Scared the crap out of her, but didn't really touch her, unless you counted the small nick and the nasty bit of manhandling. His smell, the threats and the sick glee he took in saying them would stick with her for a long time. But as a critical-care nurse, she'd seen real injuries, blood spurting and watched as the life drained out of patients. Using that scale, she was pretty lucky.

She kept repeating that, hoping she'd come to believe it.

"You must have messed up his burglary plans," Connor said. "Good for you."

"No." The word slipped out before she could think it through, but she knew she was right. This went beyond taking a television or rummaging through her wallet for cash.

Ben stared at her with narrowed eyes. "What are you saying? Did you know him?"

"No, but he said he wanted me to give him something."

All three of them swore that time, but Ben said it the loudest. "Sick jackass."

Bile rushed up her throat at the thought, but she choked it back. "No, not that. Like, hand him something. Something he thought I had in my possession."

Squinting and closing one eye, she tried to push out the visual images of the terrible things that could have happened and focus on the attacker's words. But they wouldn't come to her. With all the panic bouncing around in her head, she didn't have room for much else. She wondered if she'd even remember the names of all the men she'd met tonight by this time tomorrow.

"Excuse me?" Connor asked the question in a rough tone. "Go back a second and explain."

She rubbed her forehead and tried to ignore

the three sets of eyes boring into her. "He kept asking me to give him something."

Davis made a quick note in his small notebook. "What?"

"That's the thing. I don't know." She shook her head. "He never said."

They all wore matching frowns. Except for a bit of feet shuffling, they stayed quiet. The room whirled with activity behind them. It was like riding around and around on a carousel with all the noise and sights blurring around her.

Finally Ben turned to Connor. "Our phone connection was on during most of the attack. Have Joel play back the tape and you might be able to pick up something in the background. Whatever is on there was enough to have me jumping out of the car and heading for the apartment."

Davis nodded. "I have your car keys, by the way. You're lucky no one stole it with the way you left it."

"Like I care about a car right now."

The conversation leaped to a point that had her gaze bouncing between them. "Wait, go back. What tape?"

"Office protocol. All of our calls are taped in the event of an issue like this one." Connor made the comment as if it explained everything. As if it made sense.

The idea was like a whack to the center of

her chest. She dealt with a high level of stress in her job, life and death all the time, but she never worried about being shot. At least not until she'd met Ben. "You mean this sort of thing happens to you guys a lot?"

"I wouldn't say a lot." He threw it out there and they all nodded.

Her head threatened to implode as she worked through all the facts. "And you tape everything. Even private calls?"

Davis frowned at her. Shot her one of those "how could you not be following?" looks men sometimes gave when they thought they were making perfect sense.

Wasn't that annoying?

"We only listen if there's trouble," he said.

"Who are you guys exactly?" Her voice rose and more than one head turned to look at her, including Joel, who shot her a wide smile.

Ben answered, "The good guys."

Again with the cryptic comments. That one explained even less than the last ones about the attacks and the tapes. Still, she was alive, and that meant she was willing to cut them some slack and ignore the more controlling parts of their personalities.

But only some. "Right now I'm inclined to agree, but maybe more information would help."

Ben opened his mouth but Connor started talking first. "The Corcoran Team."

These men needed some work on the concept of sharing. "And?"

"We're a private group. We assist in kidnapping rescues and conduct threat assessments, sometimes for the government and sometimes for businesses...and others."

She wasn't sure he'd actually explained. If anything, she was more confused. And there were some scary words in there. "By 'assist' and 'conduct' do you mean you do those things legally?"

Davis shrugged. "Okay. Sure."

Now, that was convincing. She almost rolled her eyes. "Do you think this was a kidnapping? Someone wanted me or some poor woman this guy thought was me?"

Connor looked over at the police milling around and nodded a hello to Detective Willoughby before turning back to her. "We don't know yet. Maybe."

Ben blew out a long breath. "A little tact might be a good idea."

"No, it's okay." She meant to wave him off but accidentally brushed her hand against his where it lay on her shoulder. Then she kept it there, letting him fold his fingers over hers. "I'd rather have the truth."

Connor looked from her face to her hand and

back again. "We're not sure what that is yet. I'm just happy Ben was close by to step in."

"I would guess Ben was happy, as well," Davis said.

She decided to ignore that but she did glance over. A strange whirring took off in her stomach when she saw Ben staring back at her. This time fear had nothing to do with the tingling sensation.

She cleared her throat. "So, when you were at the hospital, you were guarding someone you thought might get kidnapped?"

He sucked air through his teeth, making a hissing sound. "Uh, not quite."

"He was guarding a killer to make sure his killer buddies didn't take him out before we could question him," Connor said, filling in the gaps left by the silence.

"Well, then." She had no idea what to do with that bit of information. She settled for ignoring it. That was then and she had enough to deal with right now.

Ben shook his head. "Again, Connor. Tact."

"Ignoring that, to the extent I can, how did this guy get into my house? I have double locks and…" Davis smiled at her. Connor stared at the floor. She got the distinct impression he was trying not to laugh. "Now what?"

"You want to tell her?" Davis asked Ben.

This couldn't be good. "Someone should."

Ben turned her so that she saw only him. "Locks are easy to pick. You really need a specialized security system if you want a true warning system and a chance to get away or get help."

Her stomach plummeted to the floor. All those hours spent checking and rechecking the locks. Those nights she slept in the stale air because she was afraid to drift off with the windows open. None of it mattered because any sicko or criminal could just jimmy them open and walk right on in.

Well, wasn't that terrific?

She took a deep breath and counted to ten. Her heart still hammered and her hands shook, so she tried it again. The audience didn't help, but she would not let panic plow her under.

"Jocelyn?" Ben's concerned voice slipped through her misfiring brain.

She concentrated on the counting.

"You still with us?" Davis asked.

She tried to block them out and duck the embarrassment. These guys handled guns as if they were born holding them. She was halfway to a full-on screaming fit at the idea of an unlocked window.

"I'm fine." She strained to say the words and winced over the rasp in her voice.

"There's no need to panic. You know now." Davis glanced at Connor. "We can hook that up for her, right?"

"Of course," Connor said.

She needed a minute and wanted to tell them not to worry. From the wrinkled brows and joint staring, she knew she was too late with that assurance.

"Okay, that's enough safety talk for now." Ben clapped his hands together and all eyes went to him. "No more alarm discussion. Doesn't matter anyway because she's not staying here tonight or anytime soon."

The change in his demeanor from listening to taking charge stunned her. She'd seen him in the hospital as he chased down a guy with a gun, but when he talked with her, he had always kept his voice light and his mood friendly. He had flirted and stopped by the hospital and generally swept her off her feet with his charm until she had finally agreed to go to dinner. Since that had ended with a rescue, she was grateful, but the truth was she had no idea which version was the real Ben.

But she knew one thing that was not happening. Scared or not, she needed a bed. At this point she thought she could sleep right there on the barstool. "Well, I'm not sleeping in my car, so let's figure something out."

Ben's inviting smile reappeared. "I was thinking my house."

He had to be kidding. They'd had one date and

it had ended in a bloodbath. Not exactly the best introduction for more time together. "What?"

"Not a bad idea," Connor said. "We need to do some investigating here and clean up. I can keep Joel with me."

Seemed to her they were skipping an obvious step, which was hard to understand, since hints were all around them. She held out her arm and swept it across the room full of people trampling through her stuff. "The police—"

Connor waved her off. "We'll back them up on this one."

"Why? This strikes me as being a bit out of your jurisdiction, and I'm saying that because I refuse to believe someone wanted to kidnap me." Every time the thought entered her head, she pushed it right back out again. "He had the wrong place or something."

Connor looked at her as if she'd lost her mind. "Possibly. We'll talk that through with Willoughby."

"Does it have to be him?" she asked.

"Detective Glenn Willoughby is the man in charge, or so he said when he introduced himself." Connor pointed at the man across the room in the dark suit and no tie. "He's new but doesn't seem that hard to handle."

She wondered if they were talking about the same guy. The Detective Willoughby who talked to her had rapid-fired questions until Ben made him stop. "I'll trust you on that one."

"And for the record—" a smile spread across Connor's face as he talked "—we're stepping in because you're dating Ben. That makes your safety our concern."

"A major one," Ben mumbled under his breath.

"They're dating?" Davis's eyes widened. He glanced around, as if checking to see if anyone else overheard. "That's a definite thing?"

Before they could get carried away and totally lose focus, she tried to rein them in. "Date, as in singular."

Ben shrugged. "I thought it went well."

Wiping her hands over her face, she pushed her hair back off her shoulders and bit back a groan of frustration. "I can't even think right now."

"Put a bag together." Davis hitched a thumb in the general direction of her bedroom. "My wife will be happy for some female company in the house."

"I'm coming, too," Ben said.

Davis nodded. "Fine, but you get the couch."

Ben held up his hands as if in surrender. "So long as I'm in the building."

Speaking of trampling, they went off on a tangent and left her behind. Never mind they were talking about her life. Maybe that was what happened with the savior types. They tried to control everything. Not her favorite male trait.

"Gentlemen?" They kept talking and the arguments turned into a haze of mumbling she decided to ignore. To keep from knocking their heads together, she looked around the room, at all the men standing around and the few trying to act as if they weren't listening in.

Then she saw the blood puddle on her once-fluffy beige carpet and the body bag next to it. Reality punched her right in the stomach as she realized life had changed on her again. "I don't get a say, do I?"

Ben stopped talking to his team long enough to look at her. "No."

Chapter Three

Jocelyn liked Lara Bart-Weeks immediately. She had shoulder-length brown hair with perfect blond highlights and a warm smile. Pretty and trim, and she practically glowed when she looked at Davis. Even now she made up the guest bed while keeping up a constant stream of welcoming chatter.

The place was as inviting as she was. The brick two-story town house sat on a tree-lined street just off the historic center of Annapolis. The inside had been gutted and renovated, a project that was ongoing by the look of the dismantled kitchen downstairs. But this room, with the blue walls and stacks of pillows piled on the high bed, screamed comfortable.

Lara stood on the opposite side of the mattress with a pillow hanging loosely from her hand. "Hey, you okay?"

"Not really." A thousand different emotions bombarded her, but Jocelyn couldn't seem to hang on to any of them long enough to find a steady center. But one thing she knew for sure—she was not okay.

Lara's smile turned sad. "It's all going to work out."

Rather than pretend to be fine or wave off the concern, Jocelyn slumped down on the end of the bed. She held out her hands and turned them over, stunned at the constant movement. "I can't stop shaking."

"That's normal."

"I don't feel normal."

Lara sat down next to her with a pillow tucked on her lap. "It's aftermath. Nerves bouncing around as you come down from the dramatic episode. Once the adrenaline is gone, the memories of the horror come rushing back. This is the hard part, but it will get easier. I promise."

Jocelyn still battled the need to double over and saw blood pooling on her carpet whenever she closed her eyes. Still, something in Lara's tone caught her attention. "Sounds like you talk from experience."

"Unfortunately." Lara sighed. "A time not that long ago, a man hunted me down and tried to kill me. When that didn't work, more men came."

Her comment touched off a new round of trembling. Scenes of the night tumbled through

Jocelyn's mind as she glanced at Lara. "What are you talking about?"

"I had this job performing security-clearance checks for government agencies. I'd go in, ask questions, do the investigations." She tossed the pillow on the bed behind them. "One job went wild and ended up with this mess in the NCIS."

Memories clicked together. The news, the shooting, slim facts and a sense there was a piece of the story the public didn't know. Jocelyn knew about the scandal because anyone not buried underground knew. Between the headlines and cries of corruption, the NCIS story a few months back had been hard to miss.

Then there was the personal angle. The Ben part. That was what had Jocelyn sitting at her laptop and searching for more information for two weeks before she said yes to a date. "The murders and the deputy…something. I can't remember his title but it's the case where Ben testified against his boss about the corruption."

Lara frowned. "Did he tell you about it?"

"He didn't really have to. His name was all over the papers." The boss was an accomplice in an old murder, and the boss and his connected friends had tried to cover up a leak of information, leading to a long line of deaths and Ben leaving NCIS under a cloud of suspicion. "It's not very attractive, I know, but I started with the scandal, then did a few more searches under his name."

"Sounds smart to me."

Maybe it was the way she said things or how genuine she came off, but something about Lara had Jocelyn wanting to open up. She'd hidden parts of herself away for so long. After being scared and having no one believe her, fighting off a policeman stalker with all the power and reputation on his side, she had stopped reaching out for help.

After it all blew up and she changed her life around, the anxiety remained. She battled it by limiting contact and coming up with routines that comforted her. A few times the other nurses insisted she come out with them and she did, but she barely knew Lara.

Still, the words flowed and Jocelyn was helpless to stop them. "When Ben started asking me out, I thought I should figure out if the man I met at the hospital as a guard was as decent as he appeared to be, because I've met some who aren't."

"We all have, but he is. I knew it from the second he walked into Corcoran headquarters. Not that much later, without even thinking about it, he put his body in front of mine and saved me from being shot."

Apparently that sort of thing was a habit with Ben. "Sounds familiar."

Lara's smile came back, more subtle this time but definitely there. The kind that said she was about to go on an information-fishing expedition. "So, he *started* asking you out?"

"I made him work for it." Jocelyn ran her fingers over the outline of the flower print on the comforter.

"Good for you. When it's easy for them, their egos are unbearable." Lara got up and went to the dresser. She turned around with shampoo and other bathroom essentials in each hand. "Since I'm a bit of a bath-gel collector, we have a lot of choices, but you might like a few of these."

Figuring out which fragrance to use seemed so mundane after seeing a dead man on her floor. Jocelyn didn't know how to switch the fear off and go back to regular conversations. The idea of sleeping in a strange bed already had her insides jumping around.

She rubbed her hands together but stopped when she felt a burn on her skin and saw how red they were turning. "So, at some point I'll go back to not being terrified of being attacked again?"

Lara's arms dropped. "I won't lie to you. It will creep up on you now and then, but you'll get through it. And you're safe here."

"I can't exactly live in your guest room." Though Jocelyn had to admit she didn't hate the thought.

She winced at the idea of returning to her apartment. She'd considered it a safe place, her sanctuary. An easy walk to the water and a few miles from the heavy traffic of the touristy historic district and the Naval Academy. But no way could she stay there now.

"You're welcome to live here as long as you need." Lara handed her two bottles.

Jocelyn took them without reading the labels. "Aren't you guys newlyweds?"

"Almost three months, but we've known each other a long time. We were engaged before." Lara held up a hand as she rolled her eyes. "Long story."

That sounded better than talking about murder. "Apparently I've got time."

"Right now you need sleep."

She made it sound so easy. Jocelyn knew from experience it wouldn't be. "I'll never be able to drift off."

"I'll bet you a doughnut tomorrow morning that you will."

BEN SAT AT Davis's dining-room table and spun a water bottle around, watching it tip and using his palms to make sure it didn't fall over. The edges thudded until it came to a stop. Then he started again.

Davis reached over Ben's shoulder and snagged the bottle-turned-toy. "So you and the nurse are dating, huh? A guy goes on his honeymoon, misses one case and comes back to all sorts of changes."

Skipping the groan, Ben wiped his hands over his face then let his arms fall against the table with a slap. "You held that in longer than I expected."

"You know, if you had convinced her to let you into her apartment for some after-date time, the guy may have taken you out before you could have saved her." Davis shrugged as he sat down sideways in the chair across from Ben and stretched his long legs out in front of him. "So it's good she had no trouble resisting you."

There were times Ben hated the lack of privacy in this group. They were connected by the intercoms in their watches and phones. Joel tracked their movements and each had cameras in their houses that reported back to Corcoran headquarters and could be turned on in the event of an emergency call. It reminded him of his time in the navy—all structure and little alone time. Having been out for years, it was taking time to get used to the intrusions again.

"Are you doubting my abilities?" Because by the fifth time Jocelyn said no to coffee, Ben had started to.

Davis shrugged. "Just pointing out that Dating Ben might not be as on top of things as Agent Ben."

"Feel free to go to bed. I don't need conversation." But he would stand watch. Ben stared out the double glass doors to the backyard and into the darkness beyond.

He knew from hanging out there that the large rectangular space consisted of mostly mud in the middle covered with some boards, thanks to all the renovation work Davis and Lara were doing. They also refrained from building anything out there or working on the landscaping because Davis wanted a clear sight line and limited places for intruders to hide.

Not that the guy was paranoid or anything. Though the elaborate security system complete with heat and motion sensors and a secret door to the neighbor's yard suggested some trust issues.

All those precautions meant they should be fine staying there tonight. But almost anything could be breached, and until Ben knew if the attacker wanted him or Jocelyn, or was just part of some unlikely random event, he planned to be ready.

"I'm not going anywhere," Davis said.

"Worried?"

"Let's say confused."

It wasn't a surprise that Davis phrased it that

way since he was the more serious one of the group. Much more than his younger brother, Pax.

Like Connor, Davis led by example and wouldn't hesitate to throw his body in front of any of them to make sure they survived. He ran them through drills to keep their instincts and skills sharp.

He demanded the best and gave the exact same back. That kind of dedication inspired loyalty. So when Davis showed signs of concern, they all did.

Ben gave a voice to the questions churning in his mind. "None of this makes any sense."

"Any chance the attack is about you?"

That was the worry. The one Ben wrestled with as guilt sucker-punched him. "The guy asked Jocelyn to give him something. Wish we knew what."

"Could be subterfuge. We've seen that sort of thing before. The guy fears he's caught and throws some nonsense out there to send us spinning in the wrong direction."

"It does seem convenient." That ticked Ben off. The idea he put Jocelyn in this position kept his mind turning to find a way to save her now.

"You start dating a woman and someone comes after her. It could be a one-plus-one thing." Davis wiped a hand across the wood top of the table. "I don't like it."

"You think it's blowback on the NCIS deal."

"There are some angry people out there who don't like that you spotlighted the corruption."

"Well, that's tough sh—"

Davis held up a hand. "Hold on there. I'm not one of them. You helped save Lara and put your neck out there to weed out the losers in an otherwise fine group. It's all pretty damn heroic to me. I'm just saying some of the crazier elements might not agree."

Three beeps cut off Ben's answer. He glanced around for a phone. "What was that?"

But Davis was already up and opening the small door beneath the cabinet holding dishes and other delicate things that looked far too easy to break for Ben's liking.

After pressing a few buttons, Davis took out a gun and another clicked against the table when he set it down. Next he took out his phone and talked in a low voice.

Two words: *stay upstairs*.

"Motion sensor," Davis said as he pulled out of the direct line of sight through the back doors and motioned for Ben to do the same.

"An animal?" But he didn't wait for an answer. Taking up position on the side of the opposite door, Ben peeked into the yard now bathed in a bright yellow light. Something out there had those shining through the trees.

"Maybe."

Ben checked the gun and prepared for battle. "So, no."

"Contact the team and I'll check on the women upstairs." Davis pivoted and froze.

"Too late." Lara and Jocelyn stood at the bottom of the staircase in sweatpants and T-shirts.

From their wild hair and big eyes, Ben guessed they'd gotten Davis's message on the way to bed and found clothes.

That wasn't good enough. Ben wanted them locked down. "You two need to get out of here."

"Agreed." A nerve ticked in Davis's cheek. "Lara, take Jocelyn to the safe room."

The beeps turned to a long, steady buzz. The alarm wound up, getting louder every few seconds.

Time was up. Rather than draw straws, Ben issued some orders. "You take them upstairs and I'll check it out."

"Another attack," Jocelyn said in a voice that sounded small and distant.

Ben shook his head. "Could be nothing."

"Lara, we're not debating this. Ben needs me down here. You go up. You know the plan." Davis turned to Jocelyn and his voice suggested neither woman argue. "You stick with Lara and do not come out of hiding unless you see a member of my team."

Jocelyn frowned. "I'm not even sure if I know all of them."

Enough talk. A shadow moved in the yard and Ben wanted it handled before whoever it was got closer to the house. "We need to move."

Davis pointed to the staircase. "Go."

With one last glance at Jocelyn's pale face, Ben took off. Skipping the glass doors, he headed for the one off the kitchen. It dumped into the side yard. He could circle around if he was able to stay hidden.

Tiptoeing over boards and around boxes, Ben headed for the door. He balanced on a box of tiles while he squeezed around the new dishwasher where it was lodged between the kitchen island and the freshly painted cabinets.

The place was like a war zone. He had to hope if anyone made it this far they'd fail to look around and get tripped up in this room.

When he reached the door, he crouched on one knee and listened for any noise on the other side. When the night stayed silent except for a few crickets, Ben turned to Davis. "No light."

Davis nodded and hit something on his black watch.

Ben didn't wait another second. Still kneeling, he lifted his arm and turned the knob. Slow and quiet, the door opened a few inches.

The scent of freshly mowed grass overwhelmed

the room. He waited for footsteps or signs of a surprise attack. Nothing happened.

He squeezed through the small space and waited on the top step. His gray T-shirt wouldn't blend in well with the surroundings. That made him a target, so he'd have to move fast. He glanced over his shoulder and saw Davis's nod.

Time to move.

Stepping down the few stairs outside the door, he slid against the wall and scanned the yard. He picked up movement in the shadows, over by a group of shrubs under the tree diagonal from his position across the backyard.

Even sticking to the fence, circling around without being spotted would be tough. He couldn't see Davis, but he sensed he was out and running along the far side and directly into danger.

The goal was to draw any gunfire away from the house and catch whoever was out there. To try to cut the person off, Ben headed for the fence to his left. He had his guns plus the one Davis had given him. That should be enough firepower.

He held one now as he sprinted through the grass, dodging twigs or anything that would make noise. Keeping his breathing even, he turned and followed the fence line.

After a quick visual tour around the yard, his gaze landed on those shrubs again. He could make out a second shadow and hear grunting and shuffling.

Ben took off running. Blood pumped through him and his heart pounded. Not from the physical exertion. From the hunt.

Davis and a man dressed in colors so dark he blended right into the landscape rolled on the ground, wrestling and punching. One got the upper hand and leveraged his body to the top. Then the other.

Ben couldn't get a clear shot without running the risk of hitting Davis. Not at this angle or at this time of night.

"Hey." His voice cut through the night, freezing both men.

The second of hesitation was exactly what Ben needed. He grabbed for the attacker, pulled him off Davis. The guy went through the air and landed hard on the ground with a soft thud. Putting a foot on the guy's back, Ben aimed his gun at the man's head,

Davis lay sprawled on his back and panting. A trickle of blood ran down the corner of his mouth and he held his stomach as he rose up on his elbows. "Nice takedown."

They needed this guy alive. It would be hard to question a dead man. Ben repeated the mantra while he forced the energy racing through him to subside. No matter how much he wanted to shoot the guy, he couldn't. "You picked the wrong house."

The guy dug his fingernails into the grass. "Go to hell."

Ben almost smiled at the reaction. "Then we'll do it the hard way."

He barely got the sentence out when he got nailed in the back. The hit knocked the gun out of his hand and stole the air out of his lungs.

The blow came from above. It was as if this one fell out of the tree. Might have been the case, since he'd made a soundless entry.

Something scraped against Ben's arm, and a knee slammed into his back. He was on the ground and kicking with what felt like three hundred pounds of furious male dropped on top of him.

They were all shouting and moving. In a mad scramble, Davis reached for his gun, and the attacker on the ground crawled toward the one Ben had dropped. Clothing rustled and someone yelled.

Ben took a dive and landed next to his dropped weapon just as the guy with him on the ground knocked into him. It was like hitting a wall. Ben swore as his body bounced.

That meant plan B. Swiveling around to his back, Ben grabbed for the weapon at his waist and fired up and out. The attacker on his feet got off a shot as he dropped to his knees, then fell face-first into the grass. Ben felt a burn across his shoulder as the man next to him roared.

"One inch and you join your friend." Davis's voice shook with anger.

Ben whipped his head around and saw Davis on his side with his gun aimed at the attacker struggling to his knees. With an arm wrapped around his midsection, there was no question Davis was ready to forget the questioning and engage in some rapid-fire action. Probably had something to do with this guy's mistake in coming onto Davis's property and breaking through the first line of defense.

"I'd listen to him before he kills you." Ben sat up, then winced when every part of him screamed in agony. No doubt he was going to hurt something fierce tomorrow.

When the intruder shifted, Ben smashed the butt of his gun into the guy's temple. The attacker went down with both hands to his head and yelling as though he'd lost it.

Ben didn't wait around to see what he'd do next. Pinning him to the ground with his knee, Ben wrenched the guy's arms behind his back and tightened a zip tie.

"This one's dead," Davis said as he checked the pulse of the one who had done the face-plant.

Ben hadn't even seen Davis move, but he was on his haunches over the body and staring at Ben.

Ben still didn't understand how this guy had got the jump on Davis. He was not a small guy. "He get off a shot on you?"

"I thought he was watching you but he turned before I could adjust. Good thing you rode in when you did or my miscalculation could have cost us both." Davis nodded at Ben's shirt. "Speaking of which, you okay?"

Ben sat down hard on the soft grass. Looking down, he saw blood, which led to a shot of pain across his side and over his shoulder. Amazing how injuries didn't blare to life until you got a good look at them. Then they burned like hell. "Not my best work."

"You're alive, aren't you?"

Lights clicked on in neighbors' yards. Ben could hear doors banging and voices over the side of the high fence. The siren in the distance was most likely headed their way. "I think we're about to have company."

"I'll handle it. Better yet, I'll make Connor do it." Davis exhaled as he got to his feet. He looked down at the breathing attacker, the one muttering and swearing. "Can you drag this one to the garage?"

Ben nodded. "Yeah."

Davis stopped and took a longer look at Ben. "You sure?"

"Do I look that bad?" He touched his shoulder and hissed out a painful breath. "Man, that hurts like a—"

"Think positively, Jocelyn might find this sort of beaten-up-and-bleeding thing sexy in a guy."

Ben thought back to the look on her face at her apartment and knew she wouldn't.

Chapter Four

Light flooded the backyard. Jocelyn heard the shots and bolted out of the safe room before Lara could close the door and lock them in. No way was she going to sit upstairs and wait to see if Ben got killed. Not if all of this was about someone being after her. Not at all, actually. Guns scared her and the idea of being grabbed made her knees buckle, but she could pick up her cell phone and call the police.

She flew down the stairs and was in the dining room about to make that call when she saw Ben stumble out of the garage at the back of the property by the alley. He headed for the house but his usual cocky walk seemed less steady than usual.

Through the crashing fear and panic, she saw something dark splotched all over his shirt. He got closer and… *Blood*. Lots of blood. It stained his T-shirt on his side and painted his shoulder.

Before she could think about safety, and ignoring Lara's calls from behind her to stay down,

Jocelyn opened the glass doors and stepped onto the small back porch. A wave of humid air smacked her in the face but she didn't care. All that mattered was the strong man walking up the yard as he stared at something on his hands.

He was no more than six feet away when he finally glanced up. His face went from pale and sort of blank to furious. His mouth flattened and his eyes grew dark.

He picked up the pace until he stood one step away, scanning around the yard as he went. "I told you to stay inside."

She wanted to throw her body into his arms and hold him to reassure herself he was fine, but his sharp tone stopped her. Falling back on her medical training, she pushed out personal concern.

She raised a hand toward his shoulder but stopped as she visibly assessed the damage. "You're hurt."

Ben glanced over her head to a spot behind her. "Davis is fine. He's talking to the guy next door."

Jocelyn peeked over her shoulder and was stunned by Lara's wide eyes. Guilt wrapped around Jocelyn. She had raced through the house panicking for Ben but Lara had to be crazed about Davis's safety. Not that she showed it. Except for the way she kept biting her lower lip, she appeared calm. Jocelyn had no idea how that was possible.

"Are the police coming?" She didn't know if that would be good or bad. Two incidents starring her, and they might jump to conclusions.

Ben nodded. "Likely on the way."

"I hear sirens," Lara said.

Jocelyn didn't understand why the entire town wasn't already in the backyard. Her whole neighborhood had come out at her place. Here, it was quiet in comparison. "You two live in the middle of town. How can people not be running in every direction?"

"Luck," Ben said.

"He means Davis is calming them down and will put Connor on the job as soon as he gets here, if he isn't already."

Jocelyn couldn't worry about that now. Ben listed to the side. She knew he'd go down soon. Careful not to jostle him, she shifted her weight and moved in beside him. She took some of his weight against her as she checked his shoulder.

"What are you doing?" he asked but let his body fall into hers.

Truth was she worried he'd go into shock, but she didn't share that. Something told her this protector by nature would not take that news well. "I want to check your wounds."

"I'm fine."

Lara stopped looking at the yard long enough to scowl. "Ben, let her look you over."

"See, everyone thinks you should give yourself over to me."

He let out a harsh laugh. "Now you offer."

"Ben's still standing?" Davis came up behind them with a gun still hanging from his fingertips. He gave his wife a wink. "Connor and Joel are here and handling questions and the guy two doors down who's demanding answers."

"Davis." Lara's eyes welled up as she breathed out his name.

"I'm okay, hon." Davis caught her when she leaped at him from the doorway straight into his arms. Ducking down, he buried his face in her hair and whispered something only they could hear.

The moment was so personal and intimate that it almost hurt to watch them. Jocelyn could feel the love pulse between them. She thought she saw Davis's hand tremble as he rubbed it up and down Lara's back. Heard the soft sobs as Lara nodded but kept her face tight against her husband's cheek.

Finally Davis lifted his head and his voice sounded gruffer than before. "Ben took the brunt of the damage."

Ben shook his head. "You got hit in the stomach."

"What?" Lara lifted Davis's shirt, revealing a flat stomach and an already blue bruise.

"Ribs. I'm more concerned about Ben's bleeding."

Ben waved him off. "Later."

Jocelyn could barely keep up. Each man pointed to the other as being injured even though they both looked rough.

She put a hand on Ben's chest, the only place not covered in blood. "We need to get you inside."

Davis nodded. "Listen to your woman."

She didn't bother to correct him. Ben stayed quiet, too, and she had no idea what that meant. Probably that he'd lost enough blood to be incoherent.

Without any fanfare, Jocelyn lifted Ben's shirt, or tried to. The caked blood made it stick to his skin. She hoped that meant the slash wasn't deep and had already stopped seeping.

"Where's our friend?" Davis asked as he wrapped an arm around Lara and pulled her in close for a kiss on the forehead.

The question drifted around Jocelyn. She heard it and it took a second before it registered. "Wait, who are you talking about?"

"We caught one." Ben jerked when her fingers brushed close to the stomach wound. "Careful there."

As far as she could tell, the man was skipping

over some important information. "There was more than one?"

"Two." Ben started to turn and his hand shot to his bleeding shoulder. "The breathing one is passed out in the garage."

Davis picked that moment to smile. "Did you help him fall asleep?"

When Ben didn't answer, an eerie quiet settled on the night. Sirens wound down and she could see the flashing lights and hear an older woman's voice.

None of that mattered. Ben beating someone up and dragging him across the yard did. "Ben?"

"He shot me. Or his accomplice did. I can't really remember." Ben shook his head and his balance faltered.

"Yeah, he needs to sit down." Davis reached Ben first. Putting his shoulder under Ben's good arm, Davis got them up the last step to the back door and leaned him against the jamb. "I'll find Joel and send him in before I check on our guest."

Anxiety welled inside Jocelyn. Good guys or not, going after someone tied to a chair made what was left in her stomach sour.

"What are you going to do?" Not that she knew what she wanted the answer to be. Police made her wary. So did hiding a guy in the garage and knocking him around to get some answers.

"I hope Connor will be able to head off the police so I have time to ask our friend some questions."

"He's unconscious," she pointed out.

Davis shrugged. "He'll wake up eventually."

Lara stepped in front of her husband. "No."

"He's tied up." He acted as if that explained everything.

To Jocelyn it made the whole idea sickening. "Which is the problem."

Ben pushed off from the wall and stood up, wobbling slightly. "I'm going with you."

Jocelyn still couldn't wrap her mind around the conversation or what Davis planned to do. "Are you going to torture the guy?"

He frowned at her. "No."

Relief zoomed through her.

Then Ben opened his mouth. "He did try to kill us."

"That's not an excuse." He had to see that. She needed to know Ben understood that.

"We have medical supplies upstairs," Davis said.

Guns in the house, a safe room and football-stadium lights in the backyard. These guys were prepared for anything. "Of course you do."

"You know," Davis said, "it might not be bad to have a nurse around here."

Because that was what she wanted to do on

her day off. Sew up this crew. "You guys need one a lot?"

Ben nodded. "More than you'd want."

And that was what scared her.

LITTLE MORE THAN a half hour later, most of the crowd had cleared out of the house. Police officers still wandered around the yard, and more than one neighbor came to bang on the door and complain about the lights only to get turned around by Davis. Not many people crossed him.

Ben watched the cars pull away, then walked through the house to the back porch. He stood there and rolled his shoulders back, trying to ease the stiffness working its way through him.

Big mistake. His muscles had locked up but the aches settled in. He winced in pain as the bullet graze on his shoulder burned.

He wanted to let out a shout but kept his voice low because Jocelyn was right inside cleaning up. Though he wouldn't mind having her stand close and run her hands over him again, the last thing he needed was her rushing out and ordering him to bed. For rest.

But, man, he'd enjoyed watching her work. She turned bossy and took control, which was interesting, since Joel usually handled the minor medical stuff.

Between the two of them, Ben had stitches

and bandages and a pocketful of painkillers. As a combined force, they would be hard to duck. If they thought you needed medical attention, you were going to get it.

He debated going inside and seeing if he could get Jocelyn to touch him again when Connor and Detective Willoughby headed up the backyard from the garage. Willoughby talked and Connor nodded his head. That usually meant Connor was collecting information, not giving it.

Once they hit the back porch, Connor broke the silence. "There was no identification on the dead guy."

"Figures." Ben wasn't surprised. The team rarely got that lucky.

If he had to guess, he'd say the attackers were professionals. Hired guns. That made it more and more likely he was the target, and all the blame for the deaths and injuries fell on him. He endangered Jocelyn. The realization hollowed him out.

"Gotta say, I've had better nights." Connor blew out a long breath. "Would have made things easier if we found a license."

The detective's gaze, wary and a bit defensive, traveled between Ben and Connor. "Anything you two want to tell me?"

Ben had loads of questions, and once he'd finished sizing the detective up, he might ask a few. Until then, he could only go on what he could see. Fortysomething and smooth. Maybe a bit too slick. If this Glenn had once been a beat cop, those days were long behind him. He looked more like television's idea of a detective. Dress pants and a gold watch. Made Ben wonder what kind of car he drove.

He made a mental note to have Joel run a check. "Like what?"

"I've been on the job for three months and despite your business's reputation and yours—" the detective shot Ben a quick look "—I've never met any of you until tonight, and now I've seen you twice in a few hours."

Connor screwed up his lips. "Weird how life works."

"Suspect," the detective said. "I don't believe in coincidences."

Something they had in common. Neither did Ben. "They happen."

"I'm going to need statements from everyone in the house. They answered some questions, but we're not done here."

If the guy planned to make his career on this case, Ben vowed to shut it down. He already had reporters looking to him for the next headline and former NCIS friends who wouldn't take his calls. He vacillated between being invisible and being infamous, and he didn't like either extreme.

If it weren't for Corcoran, he'd totally lose it. Connor had taken him in when the NCIS case ended and Lara no longer had to look over her shoulder for danger.

The whole team knew the story about how his boss had turned out to be a killer and a liar, but none of the guys put that on Ben. He'd worried they would see his choice to testify against his boss as a breach of office loyalty and not trust him to back them up. But they'd all made clear their support and given him to understand that they would have played it the same way.

Loyalty was not the same as sanctioning corruption. They got that. It was a shame his dad, the admiral, saw it differently.

But there was nothing Ben could do about the divide in his family tonight. The immediate goal was to figure out if the attacks now related to his decisions back then.

And he would ferret it all out but he needed some breathing room away from this detective to do it. "This was a home-invasion attempt. Very straightforward."

The detective folded his arms in front of him. "I'm beginning to wonder if any dealing with you is going to be that simple."

Ben had to give him that one. "Probably not." Since the distrust already ran pretty high, Ben decided they might as well add to it. "Did we mention there's a guy in the garage?"

The detective's head shifted forward. "Excuse me?"

"I'm sure I told the officers," Connor said.

Ben would bet money he hadn't. Delay was the only way to question the attacker without interference.

Corcoran ran under the radar. Part of their success relied upon being able to get in and out of situations without bureaucratic red tape. Not that the few minutes of questioning helped. The guy was not talking.

"One of the attackers survived." And Ben was starting to regret that. "So far."

If possible, the detective's mouth dropped even farther into a flat line. "We're going to have a talk about this."

"What?" Connor asked.

"Your team's decision making and protocol and how private companies aren't equal to law enforcement or immune from the law."

There was a time when Ben had bought into that kind of argument. Then he had stood on the wrong side of one of the "good guys" and realized the line between right and wrong needed to shift around sometimes.

"Your choice—a lecture or an interrogation," he said to the detective.

"I plan to do both."

Ben blew out a long breath. "Lucky us."

IT WAS WELL AFTER two in the morning before Jocelyn saw Ben again. She'd sewn him up and insisted he rest. Naturally, he went outside. Headed right for that garage and the man tied up out there. The only thing that kept Jocelyn from crawling out of her skin as she waited was seeing that police detective come out with Ben on one side and the bound man on the other.

That was twenty minutes ago. She still hadn't heard his footsteps on the stairs. And she listened for them. Kept her door open, careful not to wake Lara and Davis down the hall.

She paced the space between the chest of drawers and the end of the bed. Much more of this and she'd wear a hole right in the pretty cream-colored carpet.

"Hey." Ben poked his head in the doorway. "Why aren't you sleeping?"

She almost knocked against the wall mirror. At the last minute she managed to stifle a scream. Barely. "You're the one who should be resting."

For six feet of muscle, he sure could sneak around. He wore sneakers, and the stairs hadn't so much as given the smallest creak as he came upstairs.

He tipped his head to the side and shot her that

sexy smile that made her toes curl. "Still a little keyed up, so I walked the family room for a few minutes and rechecked the locks and alarm."

Of course he had. Sounded like him, but she refused to let that could-take-him-home-to-mother look win her over. "Did you kill him?"

"What?" He stepped inside and closed the door behind him. "You mean the guy in the garage?"

"Unless there are more bad guys lying around out there?" A chilling thought.

"What kind of man do you think I am?" All amusement vanished from Ben's face. Tiny lines appeared around his mouth.

She thought they might be from stress. No wonder, since the entire evening was an invitation to a heart attack. "I have no idea."

"How about thinking I'm the guy who saved you?" He held up two fingers and stepped in closer. "Twice."

Without thinking, she moved back. When he frowned, she knew he'd noticed the shift away from him.

Guilt whirled around her. Despite the gun and the job, he'd never actually scared her. She'd been unsure of him and worried he hid a side that could rear up at any moment, but their date had been so freeing. So fun and relaxed.

Nerves had made her fold her hands on her lap to keep from fumbling and knocking over a water glass or something equally embarrassing at the table. But his charm and stories of life aboard a ship had made her laugh out loud.

Truth was she didn't really know him, and the past few hours had her emotions whipping from grateful to wary. No sane woman fought off a man who saved her life. But the ease with which he accepted violence took her mind spiraling down a dark path.

She forced her feet to stop moving. "Look, I'm not trying to be a jerk about this and know I'm failing."

"You're just tired."

His hands landed on her shoulders and his thumbs massaged her joints. The gentle touch lulled her, reeled her in. She wanted to slip into his arms and forget her worries.

When she felt his breath across her cheek, she blinked. She was practically on top of him.

With a hand on his chest, she stepped back, breaking his hold. "Ben, I can't do this."

He held up his good hand, as if in surrender. "I won't try to kiss you. I mean, I want to and without the newest attack I'd planned to tonight, but the timing stinks."

She added his cute rambling to the list of things she liked about him. But the "con" list sent up a flashing red warning light she couldn't ignore. "I mean this, the violence, the shooting. Worrying you'll lose control and do something crazy. All of it."

His hands dropped to his sides. "What are you talking about?"

"I've lived through this before." The words ripped out of her, actually felt as if they tore at her throat as she admitted them. "I can't do it again."

"Lived through what exactly?"

On top of everything, she couldn't drag that baggage out and paw through it. "Can you stand there and tell me this—the attacks—aren't because of you?"

His face went blank. "I have no idea."

But she had her answer. He clearly thought he was the cause. She'd seen him for weeks at the hospital as he guarded that other man. Watched him a bit too closely, but she'd seen the practiced look before. Blank meant he purposely wanted to hide his feelings.

Another con.

"We went out and I got attacked. We came here and attackers came again." It sounded pretty obvious when she spelled it out like that. "I'm a nurse who works long shifts and, except for the occasional drinks with the girls, lives a boring life. That's how I want it."

But did she? She'd been repeating the mantra in her brain so frequently for a year that she now wondered if she'd finally fooled herself into believing it.

The best part of the past few months had been flirting with Ben. At the hospital, on the phone. When he stopped by and just happened to be in the hospital cafeteria getting coffee during her breaks.

She'd started timing her life around those meetings. She realized that now. The attention flattered her. The thought of not seeing him for days, or longer, started an ache in her chest that weighed down her whole body.

She knew that made her a hypocrite or a tease, but she couldn't stop the battle between what intrigued her and what scared her witless. That left only one solution.

"You'll get the sense of security back. We'll figure this out." This time he didn't reach out, but his voice dipped low to the soothing level that made all the other nurses sigh.

"I said no to you five times because I wanted quiet. Peaceful." The second the words left her mouth, part of her knew they were a lie.

"Sounds boring."

"One date and all this happens. You can see where I'm reasoning out the cause and effect and—"

"Blaming me."

The word stung her. She didn't mean that. "Not blaming. Connecting the dots."

"Same thing."

She reached out for the brush on top of the chest because she needed something in her hands. Needed to find a way to keep from twitching because the way her insides jumped all over the place, it was inevitable that would soon show on the outside, too.

"Some women might find it all thrilling. I find it terrifying."

He lifted the brush out of her hands and put it back down. "What are you saying exactly?"

"Tomorrow I find somewhere else to go. Somewhere safe because I sure don't have a death wish, but somewhere away from all this." She rubbed her hands together then wrapped them around her middle. When that felt wrong, she dropped them to her sides again. "And then we end this before whatever is following you makes me collateral damage."

"Happy to know you're concerned about my well-being in this scenario."

Everything was coming out wrong. She wanted to drop her head into her hands. Maybe scream for an hour or two to work out all the frustration building inside her. "Don't you get it? I'm trying to get out before you mean too much."

His head snapped back as if she'd slapped him. "That's an excuse."

"I'm being realistic."

"You're being a coward."

In a blink, guilt turned to fury. Anger washed over her, heating her skin everywhere it touched. "How dare—"

"Let's try this." Without warning, he stepped in close with his hands on her hips. "I'm going to kiss you. If you don't want me to, you need to say so."

This far away she could smell the soap on his skin. Something clean and fresh. If she reached out, she could brush a finger over that sexy scruff on his chin.

And he asked permission. It was all too much for her wavering self-control to handle. She couldn't speak. Couldn't breathe. She was pretty sure she'd forgotten how to do both. She may have nodded and she certainly didn't remember putting her hands on his forearms.

But she felt the kiss.

His head dipped and his mouth brushed over hers. Soft at first, gentle and undemanding. Then the second pass, bone-shattering and intense. Deep and full of need. His lips crossed over hers and a hand went to her hair. It drove on, unlocking something deep inside her that she'd shut down and forgotten.

When they broke apart, all she could do was stare into those rich green eyes. "Uh, wow."

"Tomorrow we'll figure out date number two."

Chapter Five

Gary Taub sat in his top-floor office in the nonde-script office building away from the historically protected houses and expensive yachts associated with Annapolis. His business, Worldwide Securities, required anonymity and more security than a hundred-year-old town house with its faulty wiring could offer.

He looked around. The place might be new and state-of-the-art, but it was drab. If his wife were still alive, she'd drag in photographs and paintings. But he'd lost her a year ago to improperly diagnosed stomach cancer, six months after losing his brother to carelessness.

Without Marilyn's touch, from the unadorned beige walls to the beige carpet, it could be any office in any corporation, anywhere in America. The only nod to the subject matter of his work was the presence of three computers lined up around the utilitarian metal desk.

He'd set up the surroundings this way on purpose. The only way to hide what happened here was to make it boring, forgettable. He'd been conducting the same work, moving the money around, for ten years. No need to change his operation now.

And he knew how lucrative silence could be. He had the expensive modern waterfront home a few miles away to prove it. He'd earned it. As a businessman he demanded perfection—in his clothes and his technology. He thought it would be obvious he expected the same of his employees.

For the first time since he took his seat, Gary stared across the desk at Colin Grange, the man who had served as his security manager for over two years. Fifty and suffering from the syndrome where his pants got lower and his stomach got thicker every year.

But his credentials, first in the military and then with a defense contractor, made him the perfect choice for this position. So long as he didn't go soft or fail in his planning. Unfortunately, this time he had.

"How hard is it to grab a woman who lives alone and maybe weighs a hundred and thirty pounds?" Gary asked.

"There was a man there."

"I am aware." Gary had been receiving reports all night. He'd gone home and come back because the phone kept ringing. An attempt to remove the woman from her house, then a second attempt at some other residence in Annapolis.

Turned out Ms. Jocelyn Raine, reported loner without many friends or any family, had a savior. Finding that out after the fact ticked Gary off.

"Then you understand how we couldn't—"

Gary blocked the excuse with a simple raise of his hand. "I was told she was single."

Overprotective boyfriends tended to muck up everything. The body count was already two too high.

Gary had spent the past hour retracing every step and making sure nothing could tie the dead men littering the houses of Annapolis to him or Worldwide.

He'd been careful and neither man knew about Gary or the reason they were being paid, other than to grab the woman. Still, that left a loose end or two. And from Gary's experience, someone always tugged on them.

"Explain." That was all he said. Colin had been with him long enough that he should have been able to pick up on the fury behind the word.

"At the apartment…this guy came out of no-where."

Apparently Colin thought it was his job to sit in a car and watch. "And why didn't you step in and subdue him? I assume he wasn't so large that he was immune to a bullet."

Colin touched the two pens lined up at the edge of Gary's desk blotter and rolled them between his fingers. Even picked one up and twirled it around. "It was a losing battle."

When he toyed with the more expensive of the set, Gary slapped his hand against the pen and flattened it on the desk again. "Maybe I've failed to impress upon you how important this job is."

Colin jerked and withdrew his hand. "No, sir."

"I have two men down and another in police custody. Independent contractors, yes, but you can see where that might be a concern for me."

"I can get her."

The clock was ticking and Colin picked this time to be incompetent. Gary figured he'd need to handle that problem, but he wanted this job done first.

They had three days. Exactly three.

"There was nothing in the apartment?" he asked even though he'd watched the video surveillance of the search.

"No."

"Then first, take care of Jacobsen before he talks. Make it look like a suicide while in police custody or whatever will call the least attention to his death. Use our contacts for that. Clean up after. Delete files. You know the drill." Not that

Gary trusted this sort of thing to his staff. He'd erased what he could find. He doubted anything else existed, but he needed Colin to think it was a matter of life and death—his own—if anything was found.

"He won't talk," Colin said.

"Not once he's dead." And that better happen soon or Colin would be next. "Then we need to come up with a solution for grabbing Ms. Raine that isn't a direct attack."

"Sir?"

The lack of common sense infuriated Gary. He felt his temper rise, but he strained to wrestle it back again. "We're trying not to raise suspicion, though I'm not sure how that's possible now."

"Why?"

The urge to kill him surged. "Because there are people involved with this job who are not going to be happy with the way you've bumbled your way through this so far."

Colin nodded and lifted his hand as if he was going to take another run at the pens, but stopped. "Right."

"And get me intel on the boyfriend."

Gary had names for the town-house ownership but there was surprisingly little to find. Looked like a dummy corporation of some sort.

That meant there was more digging to do. He wanted everything from credit reports to the second cousins' medical records on this guy. Every stone would be turned over, scrubbed for information and dumped.

Colin checked his phone then looked up again. "I don't have a name for the boyfriend."

And that fact intrigued Gary even more. If Ms. Homebody was seeing someone, people would be talking. Find the right nurse or neighbor, or even on-scene policeman, and this would all be resolved. Good thing Gary had an "in" there.

But he still wanted to check Colin's skill. See how far he could get. "Examine the police reports. Eyewitness statements."

"By when?"

"Tomorrow morning." Because there was a bigger concern at work here. Someone who disliked mess and surprise more than Gary did. "Whatever you need to do, do it before we both need to answer for this Ms. Raine and her ability to dodge capture."

THEY ALL GATHERED in Davis and Lara's kitchen the next morning. Three members of the team were out of town and had been for months. They were the traveling squad. The skeleton crew that manned the office every day in Annapolis was there, along with Jocelyn. Lara hadn't come downstairs yet.

Ben eyed the ever-present coffeepot in the center of the table. Before he could reach for it, Jocelyn grabbed it and poured a mug for herself and one for him. Straight-up and black for both of them.

In the stark light of day, Ben still didn't regret the kiss. She'd stood there babbling nonsense and acting as if he was some kind of criminal. Not because of NCIS but because of who he actually was inside and what he believed in.

The suggestion he somehow lacked humanity or would let her get hurt kicked him in the gut. It had ticked him off and kept him up most of the night.

But that kiss. That taste and feel of her turned out to be even better than he imagined, and he'd been having some pretty hot dreams about her almost from the beginning. That hair, a deep rich red, and eyes a sky-blue.

She was trim with an athletic build. And when she wore that nurse's uniform, his brain flipped to autopilot and his lower half clicked on.

Being patient and giving her time to get comfortable was slowly eating away at him. He'd wait if that was what it took, but when she'd talked about cutting it off last night, he'd shifted into fast-forward. The relief that poured through him when she leaned into the kiss, meeting him touch for touch, not pulling back, still filled him today.

He leaned over and caught the scent of vanilla.

Good grief, she smelled like cupcakes. A man could only take so much.

Joel swiveled his chair from side to side like a little kid. "You okay over there, Ben?"

Yes, but he planned to kill Joel later. "I was making sure Jocelyn remembered everyone. Yesterday was a bit crazed."

She smiled and pointed as she went around the room. "Joel Kidd, the tech wizard. Connor Bowen, the boss. Davis Weeks, my current landlord."

Pax nodded. "Nice."

She frowned at him. "But you I don't know."

"My baby brother, Pax." Davis dumped a tray of muffins on the table, then sat down with Connor across from Ben. "You'll find that Pax is annoying, but you get used to it. You kind of have to because we need him around here."

Pax leaned over Connor to snag a muffin. "I'm the good-looking one."

Connor rolled his eyes. "And so modest."

Ben noticed the Weeks brothers were alone when they usually had women by their sides these days. One absence was particularly notable, since she owned the house with Davis. "Where's Lara?"

Davis didn't look up from his coffee. "Sleeping in."

"Now that we're on the same page, we need to

come up with a new solution." Connor opened a folder as he talked.

"That's why he's the boss," Joel joked. "Jumps right to the point."

"So will I." Jocelyn smiled as if she'd been waiting all night to drop this bomb. "I can stay in a hotel near the hospital."

Ben almost groaned. He knew she'd immediately pick a solution that made him nuts. Forget running from him—this was just dangerous. Yeah, she believed he was the target, but whoever was behind this knew her and associated her with him. That made her safety his biggest concern.

"You can't go to work." Admittedly this wasn't her field, but she had to know that fact. Seemed obvious to him. From the nods around the table, the rest of them got it.

"I have to."

For a very smart woman, she was slow picking up on this point. "Absolutely not. And you can frown at me all you want. It's not happening. It can't."

He glanced around the table looking for backup, and Davis jumped in. "Not a good idea, Jocelyn."

"I have bills to pay." She slid her fingers over the handle to her mug, back and forth over the smooth surface.

He was mesmerized by her lean fingers and

trim, manicured nails. He blinked to break the trance. "Don't worry about those."

She made a face that suggested he needed meds. "How can I—"

"Whoa." Davis held up a hand "She can continue to stay at the house. Lara would like the female company. Apparently, I can be difficult."

"No." All eyes turned to Pax when he gave the curt reply.

Gone was his usual lighthearted banter. He wore a matching scowl to Davis's expression, and tension spilled through the room as they engaged in some sort of brotherly standoff.

Ben didn't understand what was happening. "Something you want to share with the rest of the class?"

Pax didn't break eye contact with his brother. "It's not my news."

"What are we talking about?" Jocelyn asked.

Pax folded his arms over his chest. "Davis, you know I'm right. It's not safe. You're offering because that's what you do, not because you think it's a good idea."

Whatever was going on arced back and forth between the brothers. The rest of them sat there watching the staring contest.

But Ben had to pipe up. "Someone took two shots at Jocelyn in one day."

A fact he still couldn't process. Men at her

home. Others following her around town to this house. He expected danger in his job. Even though he watched Davis and Pax get ripped apart when the women they loved stepped close to danger, Ben never thought his work would bleed into his personal life. Lately that was all it had done.

His father blamed him, claiming after all his years of service he was suffering a backlash at the Pentagon for Ben's choices. Powerful people sat in jail awaiting trial. And Ben had walked away from a career that had once meant everything, only to have his name stamped on the front of every paper and as the lead in every news broadcast.

"Lara is pregnant." Davis made the announcement with a slap of his palm against the table. "Okay, that's the issue."

Everyone started talking at once. There were backslaps and congratulations. Davis took it all in, nodding and thanking everyone even as his face grew more drawn.

"Why the secret?" Not that Ben knew much about babies, but he couldn't imagine a better set of parents than Davis and Lara.

"She's not far along, and because of what happened before with the miscarriage…" Davis blew out a harsh breath. "Well, we were being careful and preferred not to talk about it yet."

That explained it. Fear gripped Davis. Ben didn't blame him one bit. "Congratulations."

The only one not jumping up and down with good cheer was Jocelyn. For a few seconds she just sat there. "It's great news, but how could you let me in the house at all? Or Ben?"

Again with the theory that he was the devil's right-hand man. "I'm sitting right here."

Jocelyn gave him a "wait until I get you alone" glare, and not in the good way. "My point is that Davis strikes me as the kind of guy who might put his wife in a protective shell when she's pregnant. And in this case, he should. We're talking guys with guns here."

"I would if Lara would go without yelling the house down. I'd take her to an island with a private doctor and hide out until the baby comes," Davis mumbled under his breath.

The click of Connor's coffee mug against the table had everyone turning. He didn't slam it down or yell. No, neither was Connor's style. He simply commanded attention and somehow got it without any fanfare.

He cleared his throat. "I'm not convinced this is a Corcoran issue but—"

"What does that mean?" Jocelyn asked.

"I think they—whoever *they* are in this case—are after *you*."

"Why?" Ben asked.

"I've been with Ben the whole time," she said at the same time.

"If someone wanted to take Ben out, they could have gone after him on the street or at his house. Why wait until you were around?"

Ben had walked through that argument in his mind and on paper. He came up with one reason. "Leverage. They know we're together and can use Jocelyn to get to me."

"Together, really?" Pax asked as he looked around the room. "That's news, right?"

"Then there's the problem with the records search," Joel said.

Ben groaned. He knew what that meant and it wasn't good. Background checks. Quiet checking. It all spelled trouble for Corcoran.

Jocelyn sighed. "Now you lost me."

"Joel has a warning system of sorts set up. When someone goes looking for information on us or our property or our backgrounds, it trips an alarm and Joel finds out." Ben found the whole thing spooky but he had to admit it had come in handy more than once in the short time since he'd begun working with the team.

"Last night someone started looking into the ownership of Davis's house." Joel made a few swipes on his tablet. "Thought maybe that detective was double-checking but it didn't trace back to him. This look came from someone skilled at hiding their digital footprints."

Davis swore. "That's great."

But it was what Joel and Connor didn't say that had Ben's nerves clicking to high alert. "No one checked on me."

Joel winked at him. "Exactly."

"Hello." Jocelyn waved a hand in front of Ben's face. "Still lost."

"No one is searching for my house, which is a brand-new condo, one I got since leaving NCIS." One whose ownership trail Joel and Connor had helped Ben bury through a corporation and a shell and whatever else they insisted on to keep his name off the title. "The search was for Davis's house, where you are right now. It suggests the attackers don't know about me and are fishing to figure out who you're with and why."

She winced. "But why me? I don't know anything."

"I have no idea, but we're going to find out." Connor glanced down at his notes. "We start with the clue about the first guy wanting something from you. That means we retrace your steps and, sorry to say, tear your life apart."

Her body stiffened and she almost bounded out of her chair. "What?"

Ben held her down with a hand on her thigh. The reaction combined with the cryptic comment from yesterday about this not being her first experience with danger had him wanting to do some background searching of his own. "We need to know what we're dealing with."

"Whatever it is just happened, so I'm thinking this is about the last month, if it's about me at all."

Interesting how she defined the time parameter. Ben knew that meant something. There was something in her past she wanted to hide. With his personality, that was exactly where he now wanted to dig.

She deserved privacy, and a part of him wanted to discover things about her normally, like non-agents did. Over meals and while watching movies on the couch.

But life had been rapid-firing disasters at them from the beginning. He couldn't figure out how to slow it all down now and double back.

And her past could hold the key to what was happening today. The way Joel eyed her, Ben knew he planned to call upon all of his search skills, which were considerable, to hunt this one down.

Ben wanted to be the one to find whatever was to be found about her. Give her some dignity in not having the whole group know, if that was her preference. So, he'd try to get answers from her, and if that failed, he'd step carefully and keep the search narrow. He owed her that.

"We'll circle back to what we need to check in your past later." Connor's gaze traveled over the table. "You know what else this means, right? We're on lockdown protocol. Pax and Kelsey move in with Davis and Lara."

That was how the system worked. It was one of the many fail-safes they put in place. They drew in close, making it difficult for anyone to grab one of them. Ben was surprised Connor wasn't insisting they all bunk with him. That was the usual rule.

More than likely had something to do with the pregnancy announcement. Lara would want to be home and tough-guy Davis would do backflips to make it happen. Connor's decision to carve out an exception allowed them all to skip the arguing step.

Jocelyn leaned closer to Ben. "Who's Kelsey?"

"Pax's live-in girlfriend."

Pax groaned. "She's going to love this."

"You want her safe," Connor pointed out.

"And she'll insist on opening her store." Jocelyn opened her mouth, but before she could ask, Pax filled in the blanks. "She owns a coffee shop not far from the City Dock. We live above it."

Connor's hand balled into a fist. "No one goes to work unless you're working at the Corcoran offices."

"Wait a second." Jocelyn pushed back her chair and stood. "Stop."

Joel smiled. "I'm surprised you waited until now to jump in and say that."

"I have nursing shifts. I can't just disappear or fall out of rotation."

Joel's grin didn't lessen one bit. "Use the excuse that you were attacked at home."

"Since it's true," Davis said.

They were using the wrong strategy. Ben had been negotiating meals with this woman for weeks. She'd stick up for others before she did for herself. He had finally got her to say yes to a date when he pointed out the hospital staff had taken up a pool to see how many times he'd get shot down. He had no trouble using pity for the first date. After that, pity was off the table.

But the reality was, he wasn't the only one on that side of the table with a rescue complex. "If someone is after you, they could follow you right to the hospital floor and endanger patients, other nurses, innocent visitors checking on sick relatives."

Joel made an explosion sound. "And he goes right for the gut shot."

She sat down hard. Clenched her teeth together, looking as if she wanted to yell at Ben for taking that route. "That's not cool."

He didn't budge. Didn't give her a way out of lessening the possible tragic outcome. If anything, he was tempted to start listing all sorts of horrible things that could go wrong. "But it's true."

She saved them all from hearing more. "Impressive argument…and also a winning one."

"I had a few hours last night to work on it." Long hours of not sleeping and a few worrying she'd shimmy out the window to avoid him this morning.

"That's enough information on your nighttime activities." Keeping his caffeine addiction up and running, Connor reached for the coffeepot again. "Joel will take the crash pad on the third floor of my place. Ben and Jocelyn will be on the second floor with me. All in separate bedrooms, of course."

Jocelyn rubbed her temples with her thumbs. "A lot of decisions are being made for me and no one is bothering to ask me."

And Ben could tell she was not pleased about that. It was another thing he'd learned. She was independent and any suggestion of needing to be coddled didn't go over well.

He liked that about her. The spirit. The way he first saw the dedicated nurse and welcoming smile, then the backbone underneath, won him over.

"It's for your own protection," Connor said.

Ben winced over the monotone delivery.

Jocelyn went a step further. "Do you know anything about women?"

"My wife would probably say no."

Jocelyn's gaze went to Connor's ring finger and the slim band he wore. "You have a wife?"

"She's out of town."

Not a good subject. Ben had forgotten to warn her on this one. Jana had been MIA for months now. Connor talked about a sick aunt and then about some work she needed to do out of town. Neither excuse sounded all that compelling.

They all liked Jana. She was warm and smart. She did some work with them and supported them all by opening her home and never complaining. But those last few weeks before she left had been rough. She'd turned quiet, as if her spirit was broken.

Now Connor kept up the pretense but they'd all come to the conclusion Connor and Jana had separated. Maybe Connor hadn't come to grips with it, but it seemed real. And the lack of communication from her couldn't be a good sign.

As if sensing the tension in the room, Jocelyn switched topics. "Oh, just so you know, I pretty much hate the protect-the-girlies argument."

Connor nodded. "I'll take that under advisement."

With the fight over, she slumped back in her chair. "Okay, I'll agree to most, but I go to work tomorrow to straighten out shifts and get coverage and do a last check on my patients."

Ben wasn't agreeing to that one. "No."

She didn't concede. "This is not a negotiation."

She was tight-lipped, her eyes flashing with fire. More than likely he'd spend every hour battling her on this one. It was a bad idea and he'd drive her insane, but if that was what it took to get her to turn in the paperwork, fine. "Then I go with you."

The color rushed out of her face. "You know that can't happen."

Now, that was insulting. "Take it or leave it."

"Where exactly do you plan to stand during surgery?" Pax asked.

Ben had forgotten they were all there, listening. Breathing so quietly they blended into the background. No one dropped a mug. None of the chairs squeaked. Complete silence was quite the feat for this noisy group.

He'd bang their heads together later. Right now he needed to make a point, even if he said it through gritted teeth and the words stung. "You're reassessing our dating life, fine. Well, not fine but not a topic for this meeting."

Her mouth dropped open. "Ben—"

"But no matter what, you get a bodyguard. You don't move without me being right there." And he would figure out how to spin that into more dates and, eventually, into an invitation to her bed.

She blinked what looked like fifty times. "That's ridiculous."

"It's what we do. I'm good at my job and I'm the only option you get." He said it like an order and hoped she wouldn't come firing back at him.

After all, it was not as if he'd tie her to the chair. She could leave. He just needed her to think she shouldn't. Because, really, she shouldn't. Not with the danger lurking out there.

"It's settled." Connor reached for a muffin. "See how easy that was?"

Chapter Six

Gary walked across the small park to the slim strip of land between the overhang of trees. The path led to the bike trail and a bench. He ignored the sun burning into his back through his dress shirt and fought the urge to loosen his tie. It was like standing in front of a hair dryer on full blast. Branches swayed and leaves rustled in the warm breeze but everything grew sticky. And Gary hated being uncomfortable.

This qualified as a ridiculous meeting place, out in the open in the middle of the afternoon. But Kent Beane had insisted, and the nervous bobble in his voice and the fact that he used the phone, which he'd been explicitly instructed never to do, had Gary reluctantly agreeing.

He sat at the opposite end of the bench and folded his hands on his lap. "You run a bank. You should be there."

"I got your message this morning."

Ah, yes. The order to turn over Jocelyn Raine's

bank statements and any other information at Kent's disposal for use in tracking down this mysterious boyfriend. Gary had to admit the note he had left on Kent's desk had been…heated, what with the threats and a lengthy description of the knife work he wanted to try.

Not that Gary regretted it. They had an annoying loose end and he wanted it tied off. "About that. I would remind you time is running out."

"We're on schedule."

"Yet you continue to fumble around. Makes me wonder if you really love your wife." The woman tied up and lying in a box in a warehouse a few exits down the highway. Once Gary had her, Kent had been more than willing to unlock his bank's door, open his records and share resources.

With a sharp intake of breath, Kent swiveled around to face Gary. Fear radiated off him. "You promised you wouldn't hurt her."

"I never said that." Gary could almost smell the desperation pouring off the man.

Gary looked into the trees in the distance and focused on the job ahead. On his revenge.

They had killed his brother by failing to notify him in time and now Gary would burn it all down.

"I've done everything you asked." Kent was pleading now.

The mix of panic and begging made Gary

ready to end the meeting. "Except control your employees."

"Where is Pamela?"

Dead. "You don't really want to know."

The teller had had the misfortune to be in the wrong place and overhear too much. She should have been home that night a week ago since the bank had long since closed. But she'd gotten locked in when she hung back to check some financial records, fishing for transactions about her friend's cheating husband.

A privacy violation and reason to be fired for sure, but that didn't bother Gary. Maybe it was even a decent thing for her to do, but her nosiness had proved to be her undoing when she'd been found listening at the door to his private after-hours conversation with Kent.

It was a good thing he had thought to check the bank's security cameras. Gary hooked into Kent's system because that was part of the deal. He checked older video files because he worried Kent might get heroic and call in law enforcement. Then Gary had seen Pamela sneaking around and overhearing things that were not her business.

He'd kept scrolling and stopped at the next morning. Not knowing what she'd done, he walked into the bank during regular office hours and went to her station. Shock rolled over her face. Panic. Then he knew she recognized his voice from the meeting the night before.

That would have been bad enough to require her to be killed, but she had compounded the problem by handing a note to Jocelyn Raine. The person behind him in line. Now both women would die.

But first Gary needed to know what the note said and how much this Jocelyn woman knew about what was really happening in the building next to the bank.

"It's possible Pamela never tipped off the Raine woman." Kent had made that argument many times.

Gary ignored every one. He would not take the risk after setting up the operation and being so close to pulling it off. "I saw the security tape. She handed something to Jocelyn Raine. Your Pamela saw me and panicked, which was smart on her part."

"It could have been a receipt."

"Then there's the problem where Ms. Raine didn't exist until recently." Between the annoying detail of her lack of a history before a year ago and her ability to evade trained mercenaries, Gary needed her caught. "Put those facts together and my partner is concerned. I am concerned. That means you, Kent, need to be concerned."

"If she was going to call the police, they'd be here."

"Or they'd be waiting to catch us doing something illegal." Catch them transferring the money and releasing the data.

"But—"

"So far, we've done nothing." Gary remembered the dead bodies starting to litter the ground. "Well, almost nothing."

"You killed Pamela."

Gary once again glanced around to make sure they were alone in the secluded area running between the noisy park and the baseball field. "You should be more concerned about me killing Sharon."

"Please, let my wife go." Tears filled his eyes as Kent wrung his hands together. "I'm doing everything you want."

"She is pretty." Gary hadn't bothered to notice if she was or not.

"Don't touch her," Kent said in an unusual burst of strength. He shifted around, crossing his legs then letting them fall down. He was a breathing bundle of nerves.

Which was why Gary had blocked cell-phone signals to the spot and carried a handy little device to pick up on listening devices. Kent was clean. An embarrassing wreck, but not taping this conversation. "You are not in a position to give orders."

"I need a few more days."

Not possible. "You have one. I'd work fast if I were you."

"I'm getting everything in place."

"That's good because your Sharon is running out of time…and air." Gary stood up and started walking, leaving the man sobbing behind him.

JOCELYN STOOD AT the nurses' station, scribbling notes in a folder. This was the one cleanup day she'd been granted before the team put her in hiding…or whatever they were doing. She'd spent a year of her life not being free to do what she wanted when she wanted. She'd vowed never to go back to that place, yet here she was.

She felt a presence right behind her. The body heat. The scent she recognized and could call up in her memory without trouble.

She didn't bother turning around because she knew who hovered. "Ben, you're making people nervous."

"You're alive. That's all that matters to me."

This time she did peek over her shoulder. Nurses and doctors shuffled in and out of the confined space in the middle of the hallway. An older woman stood a few doors down, crying while someone who looked as if he could be her son held her.

The harsh lighting, the smells of antiseptic and floor cleaner, the constant squawk from the speakers—Jocelyn let it all fall over her. It was familiar and cleansing. She thrived on the energy and no longer broke apart at every lost soul. She'd hardened because she had to, but in private she mourned each death.

Ben scanned the floor, his gaze never stopping on one thing. Some of the nurses had the opposite problem and kept sneaking glances at him. When a male nurse dragged a cart down the hall past them, Ben crowded in closer.

She fought off a smile. "I can see we need to talk about personal space."

"I'm not hanging back and pretending I don't know you, so don't ask." He made eye contact, focusing the intensity he used to guard directly on her. "Most of these people have seen me before anyway."

"Sitting in a chair next to a coma patient."

Ben put a hand under her elbow and guided her to the small lounge area just down the hall. The room smelled musty and magazines spilled over every table. The television on the wall provided twenty-four-hour news coverage but no one was in there right now to watch it.

"Point is, I was on this floor on the assignment where we met. There are no surprises here," he said.

"I wouldn't say that." She noticed he hadn't let go. His touch was gentle and strangely reassuring. It also silently stated he wanted her right there.

The mix of commanding and charming continued to confuse her. Her stalker had possessed that. He could convince anyone, including his commanding officer, of his innocence while attacking her in private.

She assumed that was how it worked. The evil side was real and a guy like that could turn off the other side at will. But with Ben she hadn't seen evil and she wondered if it lurked under there somewhere.

Some of the strain left his face as he continued to stare at her. "Look, I get that you're scared."

He didn't even understand what had her emotions knocking around like Ping-Pong balls. "Which Ben is the real Ben?"

He frowned. "Excuse me?"

"The sweet-talker or the grumpy one who likes to issue orders?"

"Both." He hadn't even taken a second to think about it.

For some reason the answer eased some of her anxiety. "Well, at least that's honest."

He moved his hands to his trim hips. "Fill me in on what we're talking about."

She waited until the group of teenagers walking by in the hall and arguing about baseball scores moved on and then lowered her voice. "You change from one minute to the next."

He shrugged. "It's a job hazard."

That was exactly her fear. "Is that really your answer?"

"Do you know anyone who's happy all the time?"

"Are you kidding?" She threw her arms out wide and moved in a semicircle. "Do you see where you're standing?"

"The last year pretty much sucked. I had this job…" He blew out a tortured breath. "Well, it doesn't matter."

"NCIS." It was the one topic they'd always danced around. Through the getting-to-know-you talks and dinner, he had filled her in about work but only in general terms. More about older days in the navy and how he felt about service.

The light left his eyes. "I'm guessing you know the worst and have made up your mind about what happened and what I should have done."

She treaded carefully. She knew this one stung. From everything she'd read, he had taken on a horrible situation like an expert, like everyone should want him to do—with dignity and honor—and then got clobbered for it. His father, some military bigwig, had given a ridiculous quote about how "these things" should be handled internally.

Seeing the pain etched on every line of Ben's face made her ache for him. "Not to make things worse for you on this subject, but doesn't everyone? But you saved people. Lara told me you saved her."

"No, Davis and Pax did that. Pax has the bullet wound to prove it."

"I remember Pax from the hospital." Patients' faces sometimes ran together, but his had triggered her memory as soon as he'd said who he was yesterday. He'd been guarded around the clock and demanded to be released almost from the minute his back hit the bed.

"That sort of thing changes you. You think you know the rules and the parameters are clear, then something shakes what you believe in." Ben's gaze went to the window for a second before coming back to her. "You come face-to-face with what you think is the end, with the destruction of all you've worked for, and you can't walk away unscathed."

He was finally talking, and when he stopped, she held her breath waiting for more. "You believed in your boss."

"I believed in the system and in NCIS and lost all of it. People went to prison, but I went before an administrative board and got sanctioned for working without permission with the Corcoran Team to get the truth out. Had to listen to threats about betraying my country."

An icy cold washed through her at his words and flat tone. "What?"

"After being so sure and being so wrong, my perspective is off." His eyes closed for the briefest of moments before reopening with the dullness gone. "I worry I'll mess up. Guilt eats at me and fear tears me up."

Something in the way he held his body stiffly and his eyes drilled into her as if trying to will her to believe and accept had her resting a hand against his firm chest. "I can't imagine you being afraid of anything."

His hand covered hers. "Only an idiot doesn't know fear. It's how you work through it that matters."

"You honestly believe that?"

"Yes." Voices sounded in the hallway and he glanced over her shoulder to watch another group pass by.

The buzz of activity didn't diminish. A constant stream of calls sounded over the intercom. Still, her entire focus stayed on the compelling man in front of her.

"I've been stationed overseas and served on ships. After putting my life on the line over and over, I walked into a room and wanted to put a bullet through a man I once respected, a man who worked his way to the top of NCIS." He gave her fingers a squeeze before dropping his hand. "So, yeah, I believe in a healthy dose of fear."

The words made a difference. Him opening up, sharing and not holding back. His thoughts about danger and his honesty, even though she could see the storms inside him were ripping him apart.

She'd known fear. She had stood at her door and watched a policeman smash it down. She had listened when he told his superiors lies about how they'd been dating and had a small fight. He'd been a neighbor, then he became a nuisance when he wouldn't leave her alone and started commenting on her dates and her clothes.

He had built this fantasy about the two of them and sold it to everyone, until she never felt safe. Then one time he had gone so far that even his loyal partner had broken his silence.

No, Ben was nothing like Ethan Reynolds. Nothing at all.

She inhaled deeply and took the plunge. "Want to buy me a cup of coffee?"

The darkness cleared from Ben's face and that tempting grin slipped into place. "Now, there's a change of topic."

"Seems to me you've earned the right to move on from your past. A bunch of idiots on some board of review might have judged you one way.

Everyone else sees you for the hero you are, or at least the ones that matter do. Me included."

He smiled. "You know how sexy that is, right?"

The scruff, the bright smile, those shoulders. Yeah, no question she was going down for the count. "What?"

"Acceptance."

Right answer.

To keep from jumping on him and trying another kiss right there, where people worried, prayed and mourned, she stepped back. "So, how about that coffee?"

He winked at her. "Sounds like a second date to me."

"Don't push your luck."

Chapter Seven

Ben held the door open for Jocelyn as they left the cafeteria. When he realized she matched her stride to his, he slowed down. Longer legs meant he ate up more space and he didn't want her running. The goal was to stay steady and keep her safe. Calm didn't hurt, either.

The thud of their shoes supplied the only noise between them. People passed and conversations swirled around them as the clanking of silverware from the cafeteria faded behind them. He hadn't said much. Well, not after verbally spilling his guts out upstairs.

He swore under his breath, unable to understand his uncharacteristic lack of control. He had no idea why he had gone off on the tangent or told her so much. He'd never been one to talk just because.

With his upbringing, he had learned to hold things in and overcome them. No whining. That was his father's motto. His father had not exactly been the cuddly type, and Mom dying before Ben hit elementary school hadn't loosened the guy up.

If Jocelyn wasn't afraid of him before, she would be now. Ben wondered if maybe she should be.

Every time he thought he'd found his emotional footing, something new knocked him off-balance. A follow-up story about the pending trial. Something his father said to the press. The way people looked at him when he walked down the street. He saved it up, didn't talk about it, but something about her icy blue eyes and the way they saw through him had him opening up.

She played with the lid of her cup, tracing her fingers around the outside rim. "You okay?"

Great, he could tell by the careful placement of her words she was back to pity. Just what he didn't want. "I believe it's my job to ask those questions."

She smiled up at him. "The bodyguard thing."

"That's why you're tolerating me, right?" Man, he wanted her to deny it. But if she mentioned the kiss, he'd be all over her, and that was a level of unprofessionalism that could get them both killed.

She shook her head instead. "Just keep walking."

He pulled her closer to him, pinning them against the wall as a large group of what looked like family passed in almost a straight line. They took up much of the wide space and didn't seem to care. Since the move gave him a second to be squished next to her, he wasn't complaining.

They started moving again. "Yes, ma'am."

"I like the sound of that."

He'd spent a lifetime saying it. The words rolled off his tongue without thinking now. "Came with the uniform."

"There's a reason women love those, you know."

He thought about the one in his closet and seriously considered offering to model it for her. He'd try anything to get her clothes off in bed with him at this point. "I believe my recruitment contract said something like that. The promise of many women wanting to pet my jacket if I put on the dress blues."

She nodded as that smile grew wider. "Nice image."

He'd lived his entire life by a strict set of rules. His father's career took him from base to base, city to city. He never stayed long enough to set down roots. Some psychologist would likely have a field day assessing why, after all those years of despising the constant moves, Ben had followed in his father's footsteps.

And now he listened for others.

Around corners and down hallways, Ben heard the soft tap of shoes behind them. When he tested his theory and sped up their pace, so did the echo behind him. By logic, whoever it was should have slipped by them when he pulled Jocelyn over to let the family pass. But that didn't happen.

Now as they turned a final corner and headed down the straight passage for the more open area of the elevators, Ben pretended to sip his coffee all while peeking up at the mirror set in the corner. "This tastes awful."

He spied the person immediately. With his nondescript expression, black clothing and bulge in his unseasonable jacket, the man was very similar to the guys who had been following and attacking Jocelyn.

They were all cut from the same pattern. Probably because whoever hired them bought their services at the same place.

Finding a mercenary for hire was far too easy, especially in this area, so close to Washington, D.C., where many disenchanted law-enforcement and military types lurked. Some of these guys did solid work, protection and security, but not the group coming after Jocelyn.

"I didn't promise you good coffee." Her voice still rang out sunny and strong.

That was good. He needed her calm and temporarily oblivious to the danger swallowing up the air around them. The sooner the guy behind them knew he'd been spotted, the sooner he would attack. Ben wanted to stall. He needed time to maneuver them into a less public position.

But Ben had to warn her. Give her a second to prepare for what he knew from experience could go haywire. "I need you to do something for me."

Must have been his voice, maybe the softer tone, that grabbed her attention, because she stared up at him. "Okay."

"This is easy."

Her smile faded as the seconds ticked past. "Name it and I'll try."

"No, no. Keep smiling and don't change your steps."

Her hand tightened on the cup, threatening to pop the lid off. "What's happening?"

"Probably nothing." Something. Oh, definitely something. When she started to turn around and look behind them, Ben touched her elbow. "No."

Coffee dripped down the side of her cup, running over her hand. The steam rose but she didn't even flinch. "Level with me. This is bad, right?"

"We're going to be very careful." He scanned the area up ahead. A few people milled around by the elevator. That meant he had to protect Jocelyn and take care of the civilians. Not an easy task when he had heaven knew how many weapons pointed at him right now and a two-hundred-pound bruiser to wrestle.

He studied the exits. Elevator banks on both

sides and an emergency stairwell just beyond. Then he looked at the double swinging doors to the hallways of innocent people on the other side. No way could he lure the guy that way. Far too many chances for casualties and a low percentage of success.

"Want to tell me what's going on?" Her voice shook as she asked the question.

He thought about downplaying the adrenaline rushing through him but his heart hammered too hard for this to be a coincidence. "I think we're being followed."

He slowed them down, letting the four people hovering by the elevator get on and the doors close behind them before they reached that point. That took a few potential victims out of the way but left his biggest concern vulnerable. Jocelyn. He had to shove her out of the way and hope his shot hit.

One more test first.

They hesitated at the elevator doors. Handing her his coffee, he pushed the button. Stepping on there with the assassin guaranteed death. A confined space and no way out. Bullets would fly and the chances of not being hit were slim, if not impossible.

The man came up behind them. Close enough to violate their space but not right on top of them. He didn't shift or say anything. He stared straight ahead.

Ben kept his body between hers and the other man. When he saw the guy put his hand in his pocket and his gaze slide to the security camera above the elevator doors, Ben knew their time was up.

Pushing Jocelyn to the side, he moved her away from the elevator right as the bell dinged. Coffee splashed and the man grunted.

They'd gotten two steps closer to the stairwell when the man pivoted and followed them. No guessing now. He had the gun out and his arm rose.

Ben turned but Jocelyn was faster. She whipped around and launched both cups of coffee right at the guy. Looked as if she aimed for his head.

The liquid arced through the air. The guy threw up his hand but the hot coffee hit him dead in the face, splashing over his body and streaming to the floor.

The man closed his eyes as drips hung from his hair and leaked into his eyes. He swore loud enough to send security running.

Ben didn't wait for a better time. "Move, Jocelyn."

He gave the order as he kicked the emergency door open and with a shoulder rammed into the guy's back shoved him through. The attacker spun and his gun dropped.

A ping rang out as the bullet left the chamber. The weapon bounced down the steps to the next landing as a woman screamed a few flights up.

Ben ignored the tearing along his recent wound and the pull at his waist as he hit the guy again. Another shot and he could go right over the metal railing to the bottom. Ben picked the gun instead.

With a hand on the guy's back, doubling him against the rail, Ben pressed the barrel of his gun against the guy's shoulder. Against his firing arm.

He was too close, right on top of the attacker. Ben knew if the guy could get his balance or wiped the burning coffee from his eyes, he might be able to perform a punishing tackle or throw. As it was, he just hung there, panting and heaving, but not saying a word.

The heavy door clicked shut behind them and Ben backed up to lean against it. The last thing he needed was Jocelyn coming through the door to rescue him. The coffee had been quick thinking.

Once again, she zigged when he worried she might zag. The zig had made all the difference.

"Who sent you?" he asked, not expecting a response.

The man lifted his head. Coffee ran down his face and red streaks stained his cheeks. Those dead eyes were bloodshot and teary.

Score one for Jocelyn.

"Go to hell." The attacker no longer held a gun but he had a knife. Probably slipped it out of its sheath as he stood there trying to regain control over his breathing.

Ben remembered the other guy saying the same line and steadied his weapon. "Gun beats knife but try again."

Rather than take a swing, the guy turned and half slid, half ran down the stairs. His knees buckled and he grabbed for the railing. A squeak rang out as skin rubbed against metal.

Ben was on him. He grabbed the guy's shirt and they both went down. The bruiser took most of the impact because Ben kept him under him. Legs hit the walls and thudded against the steps. They rolled and the world spun until momentum slammed them against the cement block on the landing below.

Ben heard people talking as they walked up the stairs from the garage below. The door he'd come through creaked open above him. He remembered the attacker's dropped gun and felt the man beneath him move. Ben scrambled to his knees, trying to locate his gun, then gave up, reaching for the weapon by his ankle.

"Ben, no!"

Jocelyn's voice broke his concentration. Only for a second, but that was all the attacker needed.

He went to his stomach, then used his hands and knees. With his right leg barely moving, he slithered down the steps and right into a crowd of nurses coming up.

They screamed and shifted out of the way, but he rammed right into them. Grabbed one and hid half behind her as he dragged her toward the ground. He looked out from behind her waist as she screamed in terror.

Ben lay half on his side, shifting the gun and trying to get a clean shot off. But there was no way to hit the guy without injuring the women.

He swore as the attacker turned the corner and kept going. Ben got to his feet and stared down the spiraling staircase in time to see the attacker dump the woman on the step, then run into another crowd of people.

Out of air and with energy reserves failing thanks to the repeated injuries, Ben fell hard on his butt and leaned against the wall. He blinked back the pain thumping in his side. Breaths dragged out of his chest and blood seeped out of the wound on his stomach again. He hadn't got the bad guy but he had managed to tear his stitches.

"Hands up!"

Ben looked up as Jocelyn ran down the steps, her shoes clunking against each step. A security guard followed right behind, trying to catch her, while two more came up from below.

They all converged on the same half floor of steps and watched Ben. Worrying someone might play hero and accidentally shoot him, he raised both hands. "Calm down."

Two guards stopped to help the women the attacker had knocked over like bowling pins. The guard behind Jocelyn wasn't giving in. He barreled down, gun up and ready to shoot.

Jocelyn's gaze locked on him. Ben doubted she saw the guy right behind her. She dropped down beside Ben and ran her hands over his shirt.

He felt her lift the material and look at his stomach. He wanted to reach out to her, but he kept his gaze on the security guard's gun. "Can you lower that?"

The cloud of fear cleared from Jocelyn's eyes. She spun around, then leaned over, putting her body in front of Ben's. "He's with me."

DETECTIVE WILLOUGHBY STOOD next to Connor in the nurses' break room. The small space had been cleared out and Joel and two uniformed officers manned the door.

More than an hour had passed since the newest attack and Jocelyn's knees still threatened to give out. She leaned the back of her thighs against one of the tables but that didn't help. The blood thundered so hard in her brain that every word anyone said came through muffled.

She wanted to sit down, maybe pass out for an hour or two. Exhaustion hit her out of nowhere and the relief at knowing everyone in the stairwell was fine had her breath hitching in her chest.

The attacker had gotten away. Stumbled right out into the afternoon sun without anyone grabbing him. The fact made her temperature rise and a wave of heat hit her face, but her biggest concern was for Ben. The way Connor stared at him, she guessed he was concerned, as well.

Once again Ben had protected and rescued. Stepped right into the line of fire. For her. He had a new set of bruises and injuries to prove it. If he wanted to convince her to take a temporary leave of absence, this sure did it.

She could go a lifetime without watching Ben scramble down the stairs as he wrestled with an armed maniac. The image would haunt her dreams.

He had tumbled and fought, without any care for his own safety. Even bloody, he had gotten back up and tried to catch the attacker. Only concern for the innocent people standing there had stopped him.

Yeah, he was nothing like Ethan Reynolds. He'd proven that over and over, and she finally got it.

And she had never wanted to sleep with Ethan, but she wanted Ben.

"Someone want to walk me through this again?" the detective asked even though she and Ben both had set out the whole scenario. So had the victims on the stairs and the security guards who had rushed to the scene. The hospital had finally settled back into its normal rhythm again.

Everyone agreed a guy dressed in black had fled the scene. For whatever reason, Glenn Willoughby didn't accept that as the full truth.

"Guy with gun attacked." Ben breathed in deeply, then wrapped an arm around his middle when he tried to exhale. "He got away. End of story."

The detective stared at Ben, hesitating and giving him the silent treatment for what felt like an hour, before he looked at her again. "Ms. Raine, I'm thinking this all connects to you."

"Brilliant deduction."

"Ben." She said his name in warning at the same time Connor did.

This was not the time to take on the police. She didn't like the detective, either. Something about the ever-present smirk and the know-it-all looks. Then again, she wasn't a fan of police in general. The idea of them, she loved. The reality of what she'd faced made her question the ones she'd seen on television and in movies.

The dislike seemed to run both ways. Detective Willoughby had made his position clear on Corcoran and his feelings on outside companies getting involved in crime solving, which Ben assured her was the normal reaction.

But the detective also stared at her when he should have been looking at other things. Not in a sexual way. More as a sneer.

He put his hands on his hips. "Any reason someone would want to kill you?"

"We're working on that," Connor said.

That had the detective aiming his furious gaze in Connor's direction. "I believe I explained to you that this is police business."

"She's one of us." Ben delivered the words without blinking. He could barely stand up straight, but his steely gaze all but dared the detective to challenge.

Willoughby did anyway. "What does that mean?"

She wondered the same thing.

"We'll protect her," Connor said, backing up Ben.

The detective's smirk rose to full wattage as he turned to face her again. "And who are you protecting exactly?"

Jocelyn felt the bottom drop out of her stomach. Slam right to the floor, taking most of her insides with it. The room buzzed and she would have gone down if Ben hadn't grabbed her arm and leaned her against his warm body.

"What are you talking about?" she asked.

"Care to tell them, Ms. Raine?" The detective lifted an eyebrow. The dare was there in his voice and his expression. "I'd call you by your real name, but I don't know it."

The bomb dropped. No one moved. Connor spared her a quick glance but Ben didn't react at all to the cryptic information.

No way would she let this guy, this detective she didn't know and who took far too much pleasure in her discomfort, set the terms for her reveal. The news was private and terrible and something she wanted to forget. It would not become a line in his report or something he could play with to try to get the upper hand.

She lifted her chin. "Jocelyn Raine is my real name."

That wasn't a lie. She'd changed it legally. A closed-door, filed-under-seal case in another county, but she'd gone through all the legal channels once she was guaranteed the information would be almost impossible to find.

"What did it used to be?" the detective asked.

And she knew the guarantee about privacy had been blown. If this guy knew, Ethan might know. The reality of what that meant sent a tremor of fear shaking through her bones.

Ben's arm tightened around her. "You heard her. She gave you her name."

But Ben had to know what this meant. He was a smart man. The idea of him backing her up helped her spine stiffen again. She'd been through so much. She could get through this, too.

Faced with a wall of support against him, the detective's hubris dimmed a bit. "The woman you are so keen on protecting has some secrets. My guess is those secrets followed her to Annapolis. That makes them relevant to *my* case."

"That's not true." She refused to let that be true. Ethan Reynolds was in prison. He wasn't out and she knew because she checked every week.

"Then tell me who you really are."

She didn't move. "Jocelyn Raine."

Chapter Eight

Ben sat on the edge of the bed, the one in the second-floor guest room of the Corcoran Team building, also known as Connor's house. Ben had showered and changed into an extra pair of jeans and one of Connor's tees. Not his bedroom. Ben had slept here earlier, right after the NCIS scandal broke. He'd only recently moved into his own place when he moved from Quantico to Annapolis, but Connor's house provided security and Ben knew how vital that could be when everything blew apart.

Between rounds of questioning by Willoughby and a status report from Joel, it had taken hours to get everyone moved around and settled in.

The bottom story of the brick Federal-style building housing the Corcoran offices had closed down for the night. The second floor was alive with activity, or at least three adults sitting in three separate rooms.

Ben stayed in his assigned space, stewing

and fighting back the urge to storm across the hall and knock on the door. He'd wasted precious time tonight getting fussed over by Jocelyn...or whatever her name was. She changed his bandages and re-stitched his stomach, all while Joel watched over them. Hard to get privacy with everyone milling around.

By the time Connor shut the lights off and declared work off-limits, Ben was itching to grab her. Being close to her for hours, while she wore an overly sunny smile and pretended the conversation with the detective hadn't happened, had worn down Ben's defenses. He fought back a nasty adrenaline rush and struggled to hold on to his temper.

In the past, when he raised his voice, she had shut down. He needed her listening and talking.

Whoever she really was.

He rubbed a hand over his face and groaned. Not that he cared if she'd made a name change. He understood if something in her past required it, but she knew they were facing down danger and to not share a piece of information endangered them all. He had no idea how he could protect her if she refused to trust him.

And that was what really ticked him off. She held back. Maybe fear no longer dulled the sheen to her eyes, but she kept him at a distance. He wanted in.

He was so lost in his thoughts he almost missed the light knock on the door. When it opened before he could call out, he stretched out and reached for the knife under the pillow. A new habit he'd picked up thanks to hanging around Davis. The man was an expert knife thrower, with Pax a close second.

But Ben wasn't thinking about either of them now. Jocelyn stood in the small space. The dark hallway cast her in shadows but Ben could make out the tiny T-shirt that didn't even reach the top of her shorts. A sliver of smoking-hot skin peeked out, giving him a look at her stomach. Vibrant red hair fell over those breasts.

He was a dead man.

"Can I come in?" she asked in a voice barely above a whisper.

He couldn't find his voice, so he nodded as he sat up again. He'd been thinking about her, letting his anger fester, only seconds ago. Now he saw her standing there, curling her bare toes into the carpet as she waited for permission to walk in.

His brain misfired. Every intelligent argument raced out of his head and took most of the blood up there with them.

She walked over and didn't stop until her knees tapped against his jeans. She stood so close he had to lean back to see her face when he looked up.

She smoothed a hand over his cheek and scratched her thumb over his stubble. "I wanted company."

No way was he going to survive this. The urge to wrap his arms around her legs and drag her down to the mattress swamped him.

He had to swallow twice before any words came out. "Now is probably not a good time to talk."

Hell, he couldn't even think. Seeing her, smelling her, having her so close he could touch her made his lower half pound with need.

That thumb skimmed over his bottom lip and she gave him a small smile. "Good."

Before he could mentally recite the alphabet or come up with mundane conversation, she lowered her head and her hair cascaded around her. It brushed over his cheek as she dipped in close and captured his mouth with hers.

There was nothing subtle about that kiss. She held the back of his neck and kept him close as her lips moved over his. When she lifted her head, he sat up straighter and brought her back down to him again.

His hands slid up the outsides of her bare thighs. Her skin warmed under his fingertips and his head pounded as he outlined the lean muscle running up her legs. Smooth and silky, as sexy as he'd fantasized she'd be.

She broke off the kiss and stared down at him with half-closed eyes. "Let me stay."

The request shot through him and his erection strained against the back of his zipper. He should be a gentleman and tell her about adrenaline in the after-rush of violence and how it sometimes hit like desire. How they should wait.

He should have but he was too busy dragging her down onto his lap.

Her knees fell to either side of his hips and her arms wrapped around his neck. As if reading his mind, she spoke up. "I know what I'm doing."

"Then tell me." His hands roamed up her back, slipping under the edge of the slim shirt and caressing the bare skin underneath.

"Being with you." She leaned in and kissed his chin, trailing a line to his throat.

He moved his head to give her access, but he had to ask, "Why?"

That hot mouth licked around his ear. "Do you want me, Ben?"

He shifted her on his lap until his erection pressed against her. The move had him groaning. "Do you have to ask?"

"I waited." She kissed his nose. "I tried to hold back." Then the space under each eye. "I don't want to wait anymore." She ended with her mouth hovering over his.

"Be sure." He balanced his forehead against

hers as he fought to hold on to his control. "I want you so much it will kill me to stop."

He felt pressure against his shoulders and let his body fall. He dropped back against the bed, loving the way she asked for what she wanted. No games. No male/female garbage.

She straddled him with her palms pressed against the mattress on either side of his head. "I won't want you to stop."

The kisses got better each time. This one grew heated in a second. His hands traveled all over her, and her hair tickled his arms. He didn't care if he ripped out his stitches or Connor tried to break down the door and barge in with a shotgun, this was happening. She was strong and sexy and smart and she knew what she wanted. If that was him, he was not going to do something stupid to turn that off.

Right when he thought about rolling her over, getting her under him as he'd been longing to do since the first time he saw her, she sat back on her heels. With her fingers at the edge of her shirt, she stripped the material up and off. No bra. Just perfect breasts, round and high. He cupped them, teased them. His thumbs ran over the nipples until her head dropped back.

The sight humbled him. This was the trust he needed from her. Maybe not with her secrets, but with her body. She didn't hide or try to rush him. She let him explore her as her fingers went to his zipper.

A sharp ticking filled the room as she lowered it tooth by tooth. His erection spilled out and she wrapped her hand around him. His need for her swept over him like a wildfire.

When she lifted his shirt off, he didn't say anything. Just lay there and let her undress him.

For a second her body froze as her finger traced the outline of the slice across his stomach. "Does this hurt?"

"No." It wasn't a lie but he would have told one to get her to keep going.

She pressed her body against him, chest against bare chest. Their bodies met everywhere but the thin scrap of skin of his injury. She kissed the evidence of the bullet graze on his shoulder. The touch stung, but he kept his mouth shut, focusing on how good the rest of her felt.

"Wounds of a hero." She whispered the phrase as she kissed her way over his chest and up to his mouth.

He covered one of her hands with his and dragged her palm back to his erection. "This is what aches right now."

"Poor baby." She squeezed him until his eyes drifted shut. "I'll do most of the work."

He opened them again. "What?"

"Condom?"

"My bag." He had to move. At some point his muscles had turned to pudding except for the part of him that thumped to the point of pain.

She crawled off and rolled down those shorts. Nothing under those, either. When she turned back, condom in hand, she was naked and he shook so hard he waited for the bed to move across the floor.

She sprawled out, half on top of him, half next to him. Her mouth skimmed his shoulder, all around the wound. "You're injured."

"I'll be fine in a few minutes." He just needed to be inside her.

He felt a tug and looked down. She pulled his jeans off, then crawled back up his legs again. She wrapped her hand around his shaft as her body slid over him. Her mouth met his as her fingers went to work on the condom. She slipped it on and then straddled him again.

His body snapped to attention. Every muscle and cell on alert. He wanted to grab her and pull her down on him, but he let her keep the lead. A part of him sensed she needed to be in control this first time.

Fine with him.

"Ready for me?" She breathed the question against his lips.

He kissed her then so blindingly deep and long that his breath stuttered inside him. She moaned and he licked his tongue inside her mouth. Giving her every chance to slow him down, he put his hands on her hips and guided her to his erection.

Their bodies took over then. She slid down, her mouth opening and her eyes growing wide as she took him inch by slow, aching inch. When he was finally completely inside her, he threw his head back against the pillows and clamped down hard to keep from thrusting. His body pulled tight and his muscles strained.

She brushed her mouth over his ear. "Ben?"

"Huh." That was all he could say.

She smiled against his skin. "I need you to move."

JOCELYN STARED UP at the ceiling. They'd made love twice and the time ticked somewhere past one in the morning. The pale yellow light of the lamp on the dresser gave the room a soft glow. So did the heavy breathing of the man snuggled against her with his face tucked in her hair and arm balanced across her stomach.

She'd made a choice tonight. The right one. Thanks to everything that happened and the way she'd locked down her life, she hadn't been with any man in almost two years, but Ben was the right man.

She moved her leg along his calf. Even that part of him was solid. Not an ounce of fat on this guy.

His head popped up. The stormy pain that had lingered in his eyes when she first came in the bedroom was long gone. The stress lines no longer marked the area around his mouth.

Now she spied only satisfaction. And not a subtle hint of it, either. No, he wore the smile of a man who enjoyed sleeping with her.

Seemed only fair, since he looked at her and a healing warmth spread through her, relaxing every limb. Her body still tingled from the kissing and the touching.

Somewhere deep inside her, a light danced. He'd let her lead. Let her control their first time together. She had no idea how he knew, but he had, and that freedom to explore made her want to stay right where she was.

"Abigail Wyndam."

He shifted slightly and frowned. "What?"

"That's my real name."

He pushed up on an elbow and balanced his upper body over hers. When he winced, she pushed him onto his back and came up over his chest.

"Your injury." She whispered the reminder.

"Are you sure you want to talk about this now?"

The spin in the conversation didn't throw her. He meant the name. "I was a nurse nowhere near here when a male neighbor decided he owned me."

Ben's body stiffened under her hand. "Jocelyn… I mean…"

She continued to brush her fingers over his skin, touching his chest and his throat, loving the feel of him. "I legally changed it. Use Jocelyn."

He didn't say anything after that. Didn't pepper her with questions, even though he clearly wanted to. He somehow controlled his investigative nature and let her tell the story in her time.

She'd definitely chosen the right man.

"He started out friendly, then switched to a stalker. He acted like we were dating, though we never did." The familiar anxiety started twisting in her gut. "He was a policeman, so I had nowhere to go. And I tried. Believe me, I tried."

"You shouldn't have had to. He should have stayed the hell away from you when you said no."

Ben went so still she worried his bone would crack.

She touched his face. Gently, with the back of her hands. "What?"

The color drained from his cheeks. "I…I did that to you. I followed you and didn't listen when you said no."

"No." She held his face in her hands. "Asking me out is not the same thing. I admit at first I was scared."

"The gun. I showed up at the hospital." He

closed his eyes and when he opened them again the anguish was right there.

"You are not him. You never hurt me. You never threatened me." When Ben just lay there unmoving with his body frozen, she leaned down and kissed him. "I know you never would."

His arms wrapped around her and he pulled her tight against him. Those lips went to her hair. "I'm so sorry."

"I wanted you. Even when I said no, I wanted you to keep asking." She rubbed against him and felt his erection twitch.

He swore and shifted his body away.

She touched his hips and brought him back "It's okay. Kind of flattering, actually. A natural reaction to our closeness, not the words."

Ben dragged a hand through his hair. She could see the battle waging inside of him. He protected people, and this news had his head turning on the pillow.

His hand dropped. "I want to go pound this guy into the ground."

Anger filled his voice but this time it didn't scare her. This was about keeping her safe. She kissed him to let him know she understood, but when she lifted her upper body again, she saw pain and regret still haunted his eyes. "The man is in prison. His fellow officers backed him up, and so did his boss, until the day he broke into my house for the fourth time."

Ben rubbed his hands up and down her arms. "What happened?"

"He tied me up." Her voice trembled and a nasty shiver shook her body until her teeth rattled. "He got a knife. Cut my arm when I fought him off. I can still see the blood and him pounding on me. The chair tipped over and he was right at me, kicking and yelling."

The images flipped through her mind. Just thinking about it had the power to transport her back there. Curled in the fetal position and crying so hard it hiccuped out of her.

Her emotions whipped around but Ben's gentle touch didn't change. His face flushed and his scowl deepened but his anger soothed her. Something in his fury eased the memories. If he had been there, he would have believed her.

She rushed to tell the rest. It was like poison sitting inside her, bubbling up and pouring over everything. She refused to let it ruin this night.

"A neighbor called and this time the ambulance got there first. The police couldn't hide it and the photos a fellow nurse took at the hospital helped buy my freedom. Even his partner stopped lying for him." She shook off the fears that knifed through her insides whenever Ethan's face swam before her. "He finally made a plea deal and I left."

Ben's hand inched into her hair as he caressed her scalp. "I'm so proud of you."

"What?" She didn't have the time or will to hide the tremor in her voice.

"You were amazing."

A tear escaped and ran down her cheek to puddle on his chest. "I was terrified."

"You survived. You figured out a way through it and took your life back." His hold tightened as his voice grew raspier. "My fighter."

All the pain and hurt broke loose inside her. The tears rolled but she didn't break down in paralyzing sobs like she used to. This was a freeing cry. A letting go.

The whole time Ben held her, he whispered words into her hair. She didn't even know what he said because it didn't matter. This was about the soothing tone and gentle touching.

Most of the tale ended there except for the behaviors. She'd developed them after Ethan's last attack. Her need for control and order. She'd been to the classes and talked with a therapist. She knew the subtle shift in what she could tolerate, the compulsive needs she had, had grown out of the attacks.

And being away from her house and her life

ate away at her, but holding Ben washed some of the anxiety away. "I need everything just so."

"The toiletries," he said without judgment or surprise.

She lifted her head. "What?"

"I saw your bathroom. Your drawers back at the apartment when we were checking to see what was taken."

That meant Joel saw and probably Connor. The whole police force probably knew, including that blowhard, Willoughby.

Heat hit her cheeks. "Oh."

"One more way you overcame something horrible." Ben brushed the hair off her face as he kissed her forehead. "Don't be ashamed of it."

"It's under control. I use these behavioral techniques." She was babbling now, sounding like a complete moron, talking about things she never discussed with anyone.

"Do whatever you need to do. Whatever works, and don't apologize for it."

For a man who'd had his name dragged through a scandal and even now fought for his reputation, his ready acceptance meant everything to her. "Sex with you seems to have worked to take my mind off every bad thing that's happened the last few days."

His mouth broke into a smile. "Has it, now?"

"Definitely."

His hand skimmed down her back and traveled lower. "Then I say we keep doing it."

Chapter Nine

Gary ran the computer simulation one more time. He needed to know the exact amount of time they had to make the transfer. The government put the money in the undercover agents' accounts on a set day and time each month. During that short window, the pay would go in and the security protocols would relax. It was shorter than a second, but long enough for him to grab the information he needed.

No one had rushed to save his brother. Now they would know what it was like to be hunted.

"Sir, did you hear what I said?"

Gary looked up and saw Colin standing by the office door. Gary didn't remember him coming in and had no idea how long he'd been standing there. "No."

"We have an opportunity to catch Jocelyn Raine tomorrow."

The banking thing. He'd been hearing this theory for days. "She will not keep to her usual schedule. Because that would be stupid, and everything I've read about this woman suggests she's smart."

Colin stepped farther into the room. He held a tablet and had something cued on it. "I say she will."

The whole idea was ludicrous. That a woman who had been attacked would stroll into the bank to take care of bills and deposits didn't make any sense. That she even used the bank the way people did twenty years ago instead of depending on online bill payments and other services was madness. He could only assume she had a reason to stay somewhat hidden and pay with cash.

But that didn't change the commonsense facts. "She's been shot at and chased in her home, in someone else's home and now at the hospital."

"You don't understand what I'm telling you."

The tone grated on Gary's nerves. Difficult and disrespectful. He waited to smash his security head until he'd heard it all. It would be so much more satisfying to let him spell it out in great detail, thinking he'd won over the boss, then knock him down.

Gary leaned back in his oversize chair. "Enlighten me."

"She sticks to a schedule."

"I'm sure that's true absent an emergency."

There was no need to hear more. "You're wasting my time."

"I've watched the video. She has a significant problem with change. She has to do things the same way all the time." Colin set the tablet in front of Gary and turned it around to face him.

Time-lapse videos ran in the four corners. The times of day were close and the dates suggested the events spanned exactly four weeks to the day. Gary saw the so-called evidence but didn't see the obvious connection. "Meaning what?"

"She walks in the same bank door every time. Walks up to the center console, straightens the pens and all those paper slips." Colin pointed at the screen as he ran through the list. "She comes on the same day each week, around the same time. She uses the same teller."

Gary couldn't help but smile at that one. "Not anymore."

What with Pamela being dead and all.

"I think the Raine woman's got that disease."

Gary glanced down at the screen. He blocked out the noise of Colin's talking and watched the videos. Then he hit Play and watched them again. Same walk. Same amount of time at the counter. She even looked as if she wore the same outfit— hospital scrubs.

Maybe Colin had a point that was at least worth exploring. Gary almost congratulated him for holding on to his job for another day. But that was by no means assured yet. "You mean you think she has some sort of obsessive-compulsive issue."

"Exactly." Colin nodded. "She can't help it."

But there was still one problem. Ben Tanner, a man with nothing to lose, which made him very dangerous to Gary's plans. Leave it to loner Jocelyn Raine to hook up with the pariah who took down the NCIS. It would be a funny pairing if it didn't threaten everything Gary had set up and arranged.

Then there was the Corcoran Team, Ben's new employer. On paper, they helped corporations with risk assessments. Wanted to fly your company executives into some country no one had ever heard of? Corcoran would help you decide if that was a good idea and arrange for bodyguards to watch over all of them. If all else failed, they'd storm in and get the executives out.

All fine and not too problematic, except that the confidential memo Gary received told another story. If you drilled down, Corcoran sat in the middle of everything. The team worked with the police and government agencies and appeared to have a great amount of leeway in how it operated. Weapons, locked-down buildings, no trace of team members' properties.

And if Jocelyn was messed up with them, she

very well could know what was happening and be planning to stop it. Didn't look as if she had the funds to hire them, but with Gary's luck they could have taken her case pro bono. That made her Gary's top priority.

"I'm not convinced the boyfriend, Mr. Top Secret, lets her out to go to the bank."

Colin pointed at the security-camera images and smiled. "She'll be there."

If it was even a possibility, Gary knew he had to follow the lead. "Set it up. This will be very public, during daylight."

"I know what to do."

Gary had seen Colin's proposal for handling the issue, so he knew the plan. "I'll call Kent."

"Yes, sir."

"And, Colin? No mistakes."

BEN HAD NO IDEA how he had let Jocelyn talk him into this. It was a desperately bad idea. Out in public, not far from the hospital where she worked. The Anne Arundel Medical Center's Hospital Pavilion sat just a few blocks up. If he squinted he could see the lobby doors.

With a hand on her elbow and his gun close, Ben steered her toward the inside of the sidewalk as a group of businessmen passed them. He eyed the street, the cars passing by and the light up ahead of them. He never stopped scanning for trouble.

No wonder Connor had almost passed out when Jocelyn announced her intention this morning at breakfast to run one last errand. He'd said no. She'd said yes.

Ben had watched the heated exchange and finally stepped in to agree with Jocelyn. He still remembered her bright smile when he threw in the support behind her plan.

The one concession he got her to make was to move the timetable of her usual visit. She said no until he explained how having a habit made it easier for someone to track her moves. She wouldn't pick another branch but the time bump happened.

He'd had to wait until she ran upstairs to shower, to explain about the compulsive behavior to Joel and Davis. Ben skipped over the facts about the policeman who had hurt her, telling just enough to give a flavor, because Ben still couldn't think about that without his body going into a full-rage shakedown.

Good thing the guy was in jail, because Ben wanted to put him in the ground.

The warm breeze of summer had kicked up, taking the edge of her floral shirt and causing the soft material to dance against her waist as she walked. He stared longer than he should have. And he wasn't alone. Two men passing by watched her walk and Ben almost growled.

This part of Annapolis consisted more of office complexes and buildings than waterfront. Everything was compact and tidy—hospital, bank, coffee shop and two restaurants, and that was just what he could see from this angle. Ben guessed the street grew up to serve the hospital and all the people shuffling in and out.

As far as urban planning went, it made sense. But not so great for protection. There were alleys and crisscrossing streets. Lots of places for someone to swoop in and get off a shot. Knowing Joel and Connor hovered nearby helped but none of them could stop a bullet. They'd all try if that was what it took to protect Jocelyn, but they had to see it coming.

"You haven't said anything since we left the car." There was a smile in her voice as she stepped off the curb and headed across the intersection.

He glanced back to where the vehicle was parked across the street, then looked up and down the road, searching the area for stray cars and trouble. "That's only a block."

"So, I'll take that grumbly voice to mean you're still moping."

Part of him was. He wanted her back at the house. Really, he wanted her back in bed, wrapped around him and making those noises he was now addicted to. She was so sexy and beautiful that letting his mind wander for even a second to last night broke his concentration. He needed all of his wits and none of them thinking about her body, so he skipped the eye contact and tried to shut down his brain.

He also ignored her comment. "That's nothing compared to how unhappy Joel is right now sitting in a car nearby and listening in while pretending not to."

Joel's amused voice boomed into the little silver discs in their ears. "I love my job."

"I can't believe it takes three of you and an elaborate microphone intercom system to escort me to the bank." She pressed her finger to her ear.

Ben touched her hand and lowered it again. Thought about holding it but discarded the idea. He needed his hands free. "Don't make it obvious it's there."

She screwed up her nose and made a face. "It's a weird sensation."

"You'll get used to it." There were other parts of this sort of surveillance that took longer to adjust to. Ben always forgot the audience. More than once he'd entered into a conversation forgetting there were ears everywhere. "And technically there are four of us, since Pax is handling logistics back at the office."

None of the other men said anything. That was

the silent pact. The ones not directly guarding a client, in this case Jocelyn, stayed quiet. Or they did until one of them had something sarcastic to say and broke in anyway. That sort of thing was less likely with Connor on the line. The guy stressed protocol.

"It's all here in case something goes wrong." Because you never were prepared for when things went right. No need. All contingencies and all the practices were aimed at controlling the uncontrollable or at least finding a way to steer through it.

"You always assume things will blow up."

"Have I been wrong so far?" But the truth of her words struck closer than he wanted to admit.

He'd always been careful but never been negative. He didn't want to slip to that place. People fell there and wallowed. He knew because he'd lived with a man who excelled at it.

His father was an expert at measuring and finding everyone wanting. Nothing pleased him, not even his only son following him into the navy. Maybe things would have been different if his mother hadn't died, but she had. The what-if game didn't solve anything.

When they reached the front of the bank and walls of glass doors, Joel started talking. "Okay, kids. In and out. Let's go."

Ben headed for the closest set of doors but she shook her head and nodded toward the middle ones. This was her show, so he let her run it. The entry, anyway. The in-and-out and how fast they got to the car was up to him.

Those were the ground rules they'd set and Connor demanded. If Ben, or any of the rest of the team, heard or saw trouble, they moved out. She didn't balk. She listened and obeyed. *Obeyed*—not a word she was fond of. She cringed when she heard it. He got that. The word didn't do much for him on a personal level, but this was a life-and-death issue.

Even now, in the security of the bank, with its shiny marble floor and towering double-height walls, letting her get more than a few inches away from him made his moves jerky. She walked up to the table in the center of the room and skimmed her fingers over the edges of the piles. Well, they were loose pages of deposit slips when she started. Piles when she finished.

She looked around, shifting her weight from foot to foot. Not that he spent a lot of time watching her feet. The way her skirt swished kept grabbing his attention.

"Where's Pamela?"

It took him a second to realize she was talking to him. He leaned down to hear her better. "Who's Pamela?"

"My favorite teller."

Ben didn't even know the name of the guy who cut his hair. "Really?"

A man in his fifties dressed in a dark blue suit stepped up next to Jocelyn. He wore a broad smile and a name tag. Also carried a gun.

Ben almost jumped the guy. He settled for angling his body so he stood half in front of her.

The man smoothed his hand over his tie several times. "Good morning, Ms. Raine."

"Hello." What Ben really meant was *back off*.

"Ed Ebersole, head of security for Primetime Bank." The older man made the introduction, then turned his attention back to Jocelyn. "You're a little late today."

She smiled. "Got tied up."

"Understood." He nodded at the cashier windows. "You picked a good time. Small crowd."

"Where's Pamela?"

Ben still didn't know who the woman was or why Jocelyn cared so much. He did know this was taking too long. Someone on the other end of the intercom had taken to breathing heavy and not in a good way. As everyone's impatience grew, they could get sloppy.

The older man's face fell. "Pamela had to leave town."

"I talked to her last week and she didn't say anything."

"Jocelyn, the line is moving." Not that she had picked one, but Ben needed her to focus.

"Family emergency." Ed waved to someone near the front door. "I see I'm needed and you would probably like to get moving."

Ben was happy someone got the hint.

With a nod, Ed took off. "Nice to meet you."

Ben wasn't sure when that happened, but he was relieved the guy was moving on. "You too."

"Sorry," Jocelyn mumbled. "He's usually not so chatty."

Ben watched the man scurry over to the front of the bank and grab the door for some customers who were leaving. "Even the security guy knows you."

"Apparently most people bank from home."

"Count me as one of those." Ben tried to remember the last time he'd walked inside a branch. "Ever think of trying the ATM?"

She picked a line with four people that ended with an older woman teller of about sixty. Ben nodded at the woman. "Do you know her name, too?"

"If I did I wouldn't admit it." Jocelyn glanced at him over her shoulder. "And for the record, I don't have a card for the ATM."

"Uh, why?"

"I prefer to pay cash for things and handle major transactions in person so I know they're done, including my rental to the landlord's account."

He was about to dig deeper when he caught a blur of movement off to his left. Two guys in black pants with matching black jackets. They kept their heads down and close together as if they were locked in an important private conversation.

Probably not unusual but this was Annapolis in June, which meant eighty degrees and sunny. Not exactly coat weather. And the body language: stiff, turned away from direct eye contact, backed against the far wall—it all suggested trouble. The combination not only raised a flag, but whipped it around in a frantic wave.

But only Ben seemed to notice. People walked by the jacket guys and said nothing. Didn't even glance in their direction.

Ben's gaze shot to the front door of the bank, then to the space inside the door where the security guy stood a second ago. He was gone and a quick scan of the area didn't turn him up.

An older woman walked into his line of vision and stumbled over something but kept going. Ben took a step, thinking to investigate, but a hand on his arm pulled him back.

"What's wrong?" Jocelyn turned around and wrapped her fingers around his elbow as she whispered the question.

He gave the response without thinking, with the ease that some people said hello. "Nothing."

Her nails dug into the skin of his forearm. "Nice try. Tell me."

Joel picked that moment to break in. "What's up?"

"Do you have eyes in here?" Ben kept his voice low and barely moved his lips. Anyone looking would think he was talking to Jocelyn, especially since she stared at him in frantic panic right now.

"Tapped into the security cameras." Keys clicked on Joel's end. "Scanning the floor."

A nerve at the back of Ben's neck twitched. The old instincts roared to life, letting him know something bad was coming. That feeling was rarely wrong.

Joel's voice whispered over the line again. "Get out of there."

Ben didn't know what Joel saw, but the warning was good enough to get him moving. Now on edge and ready for battle, he shifted his weight. Forget the worry about upsetting the other bank patrons. He wanted Jocelyn out of there and it had to be quick. The line kept shuffling forward and people mingled, looking at cell phones and filling out deposit slips.

It all seemed so normal, but he knew. A guy didn't devote every minute of his adult life, almost eighteen years, to service and rescue without picking up a few cues.

"Get behind me." This time he looked at her.

She had the same earpiece and heard the order, but whatever she saw in his expression had her shoulders stiffening as the color leached out of her face. "How bad is it?"

"I'm thinking pretty bad," he said as he dropped eye contact. The pale skin and wide eyes made him want to comfort her. But she needed his protection right now, not a reassuring hug. "Hold on to the back of my shirt and stay close. We'll walk to the door."

"Right."

"Do not stop."

"Robbery?" The word was little more than a puff of air on her lips.

In her stupor, she stumbled back and bumped into the woman in front of her. Ben mumbled an apology as he wrapped an arm around her and started to turn. In the whir of activity, with people coming in and out and walking around them, he saw the teller on the far end look up and go into a sort of trance. Ben followed his gaze to the jacket crew.

Now or never.

A sharp bang rang out, echoing off every surface and mixing with the screams of the bank patrons.

Too late.

On instinct, Ben dropped down, spinning as he went and dragging Jocelyn with him. His knees hit the hard floor as he took the brunt of their joint weight. Ignoring her yelp of surprise and the thud of her body rolling into his, he tucked her underneath him with his chest against her back and his weight balanced on one elbow.

"This can't be happening again." She whispered the words low enough for only him to hear.

The despair in her voice pulled at him. "We'll get through this, too."

"Promise me."

He couldn't say the words. Planted a quick kiss on the back of her head instead.

If this was the newest in a line of escalating attacks, this one blew the others away. Well planned and performed in tandem. They had doubled the number of attackers and dressed them up for show.

The risks skyrocketed with a move like this. Cars on the street and people with cells and alarms. It would be hard to get out now that they were in, especially since they weren't running up to the tellers and demanding cash.

But the fact that had Ben's gut twisting was it would be too easy to take Jocelyn out in this situation. Just make it look like part of a bank robbery gone bad, and quiet her before they figured out what it was she supposedly knew.

He vowed right then not to let himself get separated from Jocelyn. If that meant going out in a suicidal hail of gunfire, he'd do it. He just wished he'd spent a few minutes of their time together teaching her to shoot and how to defend herself.

Tomorrow. There would be a tomorrow and he'd do it then.

His hand hovered near the weapon hidden by his left ankle as his gaze shot to the door. The room fell into a shadowy gray as two men by the floor-to-ceiling front windows lowered the shades, blocking out the street beyond.

Ben had no idea where the masks and guns came from, but the men had both. And it all happened in less than ten seconds.

With a gun and a knife, Ben could take on a few of them. He counted four masked gunmen. No way could he win a shoot-out against that many without civilians getting hit in the cross fire. Joel and Connor and the police, whom Connor would've surely contacted, evened the odds, but they had to get inside to be useful.

Rather than risk drawing attention or starting a bloodbath, Ben ignored the weapons. For now. He thought about the small silver ball in his ear. "Joel, you getting this?"

"Yep."

"Everyone shut up." The gunman in the middle of the room held up his weapon as he shouted his order.

Shoes clicked against the floor as two more armed men circled around him, both with their faces hidden. They paced through the curled and crying bodies of bank patrons scattered around the floor and hiding behind any desk or counter they could find. Most people sat huddled in groups on the floor and soft wailing came from Ben's blind side.

The gunman by the front door swung his gun over the room and stopped on a businessman. "Everyone down now. Phones and wallets on the floor in front of you and no talking."

Clothing rustled and feet shuffled as the last of the bank patrons crawled to the floor. A fierce tremble ran through Jocelyn as she lay half on her side with her legs out behind her. Ben smoothed a hand over hers on the ground, hoping his touch would help calm her down.

"Get on your knees," he whispered right into her ear. The theory being, with her feet under her, he could get her up if the chance for escape presented itself. The gunmen had to load the money and soon if they wanted to make this quick, which was the point of a bank robbery. Which was not why Ben thought they were here.

Ben barely made a sound but the man in the

middle turned toward him. In two steps, he was on top of them, sticking the barrel of the gun in Ben's face. "You got something to say, hotshot?"

Ben shook his head, bowing until his forehead almost touched the floor beside Jocelyn's prone form in what he hoped looked like a move of deference. He really wanted to hide his face and keep hers down in the event the men were here for them and hadn't picked them out yet. When the scuffed shoes finally disappeared from in front of his nose, Ben eased his chest back up and ran a hand through his hair.

"This, folks, is a robbery, and anyone who talks or moves gets killed." The man in the middle of the room turned around in a circle as he talked in a low, gravelly voice. "Anyone touches an alarm or yells, dies. You stay calm and you get to walk out of here in a few minutes."

Ben looked for bags, for any movement toward the counter to gather money. Nothing. The attackers stood, weapons up and ready, taking their time and staking out positions across the room. They forfeited speed and quiet in favor of getting the people on the floor and the visibility to the outside blocked.

With a nod from the guy in the middle, who clearly acted as leader, two of the men broke off and headed to the slim staircase that ran to the balcony above them. Ben saw an open landing in a square around the main part of the room. There were a few doors up and off to his right, but nothing else up there but a walkway.

Ben guessed the men could gain a strategic position from above, but they walked up the stairs and kept going until they hit the emergency door. None of their actions made sense. Ben expected sirens any minute. This type of crime only worked if the attackers made a rush for the money and then raced to a waiting car. Even then it was a high-risk operation in the middle of a busy business day.

And if they wanted Jocelyn, why not grab her?

He wasn't familiar with this bank but he could see the door to the safe right there on the main floor. He had no idea what could be upstairs that would warrant this kind of attention from gunmen who should want to grab and run.

But they didn't run. They didn't even move fast.

That nerve at the back of Ben's neck ticked. He recognized the pull for what it was—a fresh warning. Tension flooded through him with a kick of adrenaline streaming right behind. This was no in-and-out. No grabbing of the people in charge. These guys had something else in mind. Likely something that involved Jocelyn.

"What are they doing?" She asked the question to the floor, low and barely above a hum.

"No idea."

But he knew they were all in trouble.

Chapter Ten

Jocelyn was afraid to lift her head. If they came for her, she didn't want to make it easy for them to find her. She didn't want anyone else hurt, either. She heard a low hum on the mic in her ear. But it was the beating inside her ears that had her concerned. She could barely think over the incessant pounding.

The temptation was to turn this over to Ben and let him figure a way out. He was the professional and she was a nurse who kept landing in trouble. But the idea of waiting and hiding no longer appealed to her. Those days were behind her. Ethan Reynolds could not hurt her anymore.

And after the past few days, she no longer feared a little man with a big ego and even bigger fists. She'd outlasted and outrun men with guns who could crush Ethan. She used her wits and depended on the right people to help her through.

She would make it through this, too. She had to believe that.

One of the attackers crouched down and started looking through the wallets. He didn't take money. He flipped them open and…checked IDs. The pieces fell into place. Ben guessed this wasn't a robbery and he was right. It was a hunt—for her.

She watched the attacker scan photos and faces. He dumped purses and shifted the contents around until he grabbed only the licenses.

"They don't know what you look like." Ben whispered the words into her hair.

It took all of her control to hold her body still and not jerk at the impact of those words. "Yes."

"How can that be?" he asked.

Probably had something to do with her name-switching and lack of a background trail. She had a license stuffed into her front pants pocket. No purse and no wallet.

She'd come in and out of here every week since she took the job down the street. Pamela had stopped looking at her license long ago. Jocelyn only took it with her as a precaution and she kept it tucked away now.

"Anything?" The leader glanced at his watch when the other attacker shook his head. "Okay, I need all the women on the right side and men to the left. Be quick and don't try anything."

One man got up and tripped and the gun swung right to him. "Please, no," he pleaded.

"Enough stalling. Everyone move."

Her knee banged against the hard floor as she tried to get her weight under her so she could stand up. She hated the idea. The thought of being separated from Ben started a shiver racing through her that the warm day and Ben's hard body over her couldn't slow.

This manhunt was about her. She had no idea what they wanted or how they intended to get it out of her, but there was nowhere else to hide.

She shifted to get up before the attacker got upset and took it out on Ben. She attempted to stand, but Ben pressed harder, flattening her against the ground again. No question he wanted her down.

When she peeked at him over her shoulder, he shook his head.

Do not move. He mouthed the words this time.

"You've got two," Joel said through the mic.

She had no idea what that meant. She couldn't ask, so she hoped Ben understood the clue.

The lead attacker stuck his gun right in a woman's face just a few feet away from Jocelyn. "I said, move."

People started shifting. A woman sobbed as the other attacker dragged her off the floor and threw her where he wanted her. "Let's go."

The room exploded into movement. Most people crawled on the floor rather than stand up, but the game of musical chairs with people had begun. Men filed one way and women the other. Only she and Ben stayed still on the floor.

If the plan was for him to cover her and take the bullets while Connor stormed in the front door, she voted for another plan. Suddenly her fears switched from what these men might do to her, to what they *would* do to Ben if he didn't listen.

She tried to think about how she could cause a diversion, at least give Ben a chance to launch an attack of some kind.

"No."

That was it. One word whispered against the back of her head. She hadn't said anything out loud and there was no way he could feel the anxiety churning and bubbling inside her. Yet he knew.

"Hey, you two. Get up." The lead attacker stood right in front of them now. No more than five feet away.

She ducked her head and tried to peek up without the lead attacker getting a good look at her face. She saw his shoes, work boots of some kind. Saw him lift his weapon.

"You have two seconds before I start shooting."

"We're going." Ben's voice sounded thin and wobbly, as if he were terrified and too shaken with fear to get his legs to move.

No way. She knew it was fake. All fake. Whatever the plan, he'd put it in motion. She heard a countdown in her ear and knew Joel was helping from the outside.

Most of Ben's weight lifted off her. She tried to move but his legs kept her pinned. They were targets right there in the center of the floor. The room had split and no else sat with them. A man off to the side begged Ben to move.

He took his time. He reached behind him and got to his knees, all while the lead attacker watched.

When the seconds ticked on, the other attacker stepped closer. "What's happening over here?"

The room spun. Something slammed into her back, knocking the air out of her and pushing her tight against the floor. She covered her head as the chaos exploded around her. She heard screaming and saw a blur as Ben threw something with one hand and a single shot rang out above her.

The noise cut off her hearing as it burned through her. She smelled smoke and saw people running. Time flew yet moved in slow motion. She saw every tiny movement even as she knew it unfolded in rapid time.

"Ben!" She screamed his name but he was up and running.

The front doors burst open and Connor and Joel raced in with the police sirens wailing in the street behind them. Ben jumped over the lead attacker's still body. Then she saw the blood and the attacker's open hand. His gun lay a few feet away but his body didn't move.

Blood covered Ben's arm and stained his shirt. She tried to yell and rush for him, but strong hands held her back. She threw her elbows and kicked her feet but nothing happened. The hold didn't ease.

Joel's voice finally penetrated the frantic screaming in her head. This time in person, not through the mic. "Stay still. He's okay."

"Blood."

"Not his."

Then she went down again. Joel pressed her against him, shielding her with his body as people filed around the room and ran for the doors in a wild frenzy.

Flat against the floor, she could see Ben and Connor reach the lone attacker leaning against the table in the middle of the bank. Something stuck out of his shoulder and his gun dangled from his hand.

Connor took that guy's mask off, and his face was a mask of pain as his head fell back. She wondered why he didn't slide to the floor.

Sounds were muffled and she didn't understand what she was seeing. A blur moved into her peripheral vision. She looked up in time to see one of the attackers come out of the door upstairs. He held a gun.

She didn't know where he aimed, so she screamed the warning. "Ben, move!"

He dropped to the floor in what looked like a slide into home plate. Her heart stopped when his momentum had him skidding into the knifed man. Shots echoed around the room and pinged off the stone walls. Ben slammed into the attacker's legs and the guy went down as shots slammed into his chest.

Through the fog and the ringing pain in her ears, she heard a yell followed by a sickening thud. No one stood on the balcony above. A deadly silence fell over the room.

Her panicked gaze flew from one corner to the other. First to Ben where he sat on his butt still holding his gun. She followed his stare to the pile of black folded on the hard floor not that far from where she sat. Then she swung back to Ed. He stood near the front door with his gun still aimed at the balcony.

The doors slammed open again and police officers poured in, fanning out and covering the entire floor. The direction they pointed their guns shifted between all the men still standing. The innocent ones.

"Get down!" Different voices all said the same thing.

The command rang all around her and the room headed into a spinning nosedive. She refused to pass out, but when Detective Willoughby stepped into the middle of the fray, she did lower her forehead to the floor and let the cool stone ease the hammering inside.

He looked around at the blood and the bodies. "Arrest everybody."

IT TOOK CONNOR all of ten minutes to talk the detective down. No wonder Connor was the leader. He could stay calm and reasonable and get people moving his way before they knew they were agreeing with him.

Ben would have yelled his way through the situation. With his patience expired, he'd reached the end of being social and professional. The detective had proved to be nothing but trouble. He was no help and more of an actual hindrance. Always a step behind and full of accusations. Ben was done with all of it.

Every part of his body ached and the realization of how close he'd come to seeing Jocelyn captured or killed had adrenaline rushing to his brain. With the police moving in and out and investigators roping off the area, Ben didn't move. He leaned against the middle table with the deposit slips now strewn all over it and on the floor.

When he finally shifted, his foot slid on the

paper and his gaze shot across the room to see who'd witnessed his near fall. Jocelyn stood there. He could watch her all day.

She nodded and talked to Joel. They were holding hands. No, that wasn't right. Ben forced his vision to clear—Joel was checking her arm. Squeezing and asking questions, then waiting for an answer. Ben had been through that routine a few times himself.

The images of the past half hour clicked together in his head. He'd pinned her under him against the floor, ignoring his weight advantage. He recalled the way he'd shoved her down to keep her out of the line of fire. Rough, but necessary. He hoped she understood, but that didn't stop the guilt from the thought of her being hurt without him even noticing.

He shot up straight and stalked across the room. He got three feet away when her face fell. Man, she looked a second away from crying and his heart stammered in response.

"Jocelyn?"

She launched her body at him. Despite the raw pain radiating from his shoulder and the fatigue pulling at his muscles, he caught her and held her close. His mouth went to the side of her head and then her cheek.

That wasn't enough. Turning, he held her face in his hands and kissed her. Right there in front of everyone with bodies on the floor and police-men whispering around them.

When he came up for air, he felt whole again. Somehow this woman had wormed her way into his soul and now he couldn't breathe without her near him. The realization of how far gone he was had him leaning against her.

"Are you okay?" She whispered the question.

With his body wrapped around hers, he almost didn't hear it. "Yes." He held her away from him, careful not to hit her arm.

"I'm fine," she said before he could ask.

"But Joel was—"

"My wrist is sore." She twirled it around as if to assure him it wasn't broken. "And that doesn't matter."

The security chief, or whatever his title was—Ben couldn't remember—came up beside them. In his tenuous mood, Ben wanted to push him away. But this was the guy who'd made the final shot to bring down the guy on the balcony. Ben owed him something.

"Ms. Raine?"

She slipped out of Ben's arms and gave Ed a smile. "You doing okay?"

"That was a heck of a shot," Ben said, wondering what kind of skills this guy had. Until now, he'd never thought of security guards as expert marksmen.

The shot was within normal range, but emotions had been running high and tension had flooded over everything like an oil slick. Still, the guy had maintained his composure and hit a moving target above him. Any way you sliced that, it was impressive.

"I had him clear in my sights." Ed glanced up at the spot where he took the attacker down. "I'm just happy that was as bad as it got. You're all lucky you weren't killed."

Jocelyn patted the man's arm before stepping back beside Ben again. "And you, too."

Ed shook his head. "Weirdest robbery I've ever seen."

Not quite the comment Ben expected. It wasn't what the other man said. It was what he left out and the steady tone. For a guy who'd come through a crazy situation, Ed seemed ready to head back to work without missing a step.

That made one of them.

"Was this your first?" Ben asked.

"No, but the robbers usually get in and out." Ed frowned. "What was your name again?"

"Ben Tanner." He waited for a response, but nothing came. People usually reacted. Very few gave him the blank stare like the one Ed left for him.

There were those who supported Ben and the NCIS outcome and offered something akin to praise. Those who didn't tended not to need words because their expressions or dismissals were clear, though Ben sometimes heard some awful things from them, too. Amazing how vocal the "anti" crowd always turned out to be.

But this guy showed no reaction. Could mean he skipped the news. That was the most likely scenario, but nothing about this case had fit into a reasonable pattern so far, so Ben filed the information away to chew on later. When he analyzed everything else, he'd look at that, too.

"Nice to meet you." Ed gave a quick nod and left.

He passed the bigger problem on the way in. "I hate to break this up, but I need to speak with Ms. Raine."

"Detective Willoughby." At this point Ben had his own nickname for the guy but he refrained from saying it because he'd probably get arrested.

The detective kept his attention focused solely on Jocelyn. "I would have bet money you were in the middle of this."

"I came in to pay a bill," she said.

"There are checks for things like that."

Ben had had enough of the macho act. Willoughby liked to stand too close and pin people with a dead stare. Two days ago Ben had found the whole routine annoying. Now he was done with all of it.

"She handled herself really well," Ben said, daring the other man to disagree. Any reason to land a punch at this point worked for Ben.

"I'm thinking she's had some experience."

Yeah, this guy just didn't take a hint. Ben decided to make his position a bit more clear. "You have a point, Willoughby? If so, feel free to make it to me."

"I'm talking to the lady."

Ben took a step forward and Jocelyn pulled him back. "It's okay, Ben. Detective Willoughby is doing his job and his tactics don't scare me."

Since she slipped her hand in his, Ben guessed whatever was jumping around inside her didn't match the cool detachment of her words. Ben gave her fingers a reassuring squeeze. "It's actually not okay."

The detective ignored everything except what he wanted to say. He pointed from Ben to Jocelyn. "I'm going to need a list of where you plan to go the next few days."

"Why?" she asked.

"So I can have an ambulance ready."

Connor picked that moment to step in. There was another man with him. "Detective."

"Connor Bowen."

"Are we only using full names now?" Joel asked as he joined the group.

Connor pointed to the other man. "This is Kent Beane, the bank president."

To Ben's mind the guy looked ready to throw up. Sweat dripped off his forehead and he kept folding a handkerchief and wiping his brow. Beane acted as if someone had stolen his personal bank account and his house along with it.

Of course, since no one had tried to steal anything, the guy had bigger problems. Someone had used his office as a staging ground to grab Jocelyn. That put him on Ben's list.

Willoughby ignored the introductions. "I got a call from my boss about you."

Connor smiled. "Tell Anne I said hello."

"I'm not sure who you think you are or why you're protecting Ms. Raine—"

"Are you in trouble, Ms. Raine?" Kent asked.

"But it ends here."

That qualified as one threat too many. Ben heard it, let it wind through him and feed the anger festering inside him. "Is that what your boss said you were supposed to do? Threaten women for no reason?"

The detective turned on him. "I'm betting the media would love to know what you're doing now."

Jocelyn let out a grumbling noise and shook off Ben's hand. "How dare you?"

Whoa. Ben grabbed the hem of her shirt and

pulled her back before she tackled the guy. Leaving his hand resting there, he massaged her lower back, letting her know he appreciated the support.

Not many people stepped up for him. Knowing she would meant something. Meant a lot. But he didn't want her to make herself any more of a target.

He could handle the detective. "Is that supposed to be a threat, Detective? If so, you need to do better."

Willoughby shifted his attention back to Jocelyn. "You have one day to come clean. You tell me who you are and what's going on and your boyfriend stays off the front page."

"What is wrong with you?"

Jocelyn asked it but Ben figured they were all thinking it.

"Well, now." Joel made a humming sound. "We've been throwing words around, but that statement is definitely a threat."

"And you're a bit late to throw out one about my life. I can't imagine what hasn't been printed about me." There was a strange freedom in knowing there was nothing left for people to say about him. Ben didn't find a lot of comfort in the thought but he did see himself as slander-proof.

"I'll take that as a challenge."

The detective stormed off before anyone could

respond or Ben could shove the guy through the wall the way he wanted to do.

"Who was that again?" Kent asked.

"He's a jack—"

"Okay." Connor shut down Ben's honest response. "That's enough."

"Nice work today." Ben didn't know if it was true or not. He didn't remember seeing the manager anywhere during the attack. Joel's video would tell them, but Ben had the clear sense this guy had ducked the tragedy.

Kent shook his head. He kept alternating between swiping his brow and swallowing. "I missed it, I'm afraid."

At least he didn't try to lie. Ben didn't really count that in the guy's favor, but it was something. Now if he'd just stop leaking sweat. "You weren't in the room?"

"Stepped out for coffee. Dropped it all over the street when I saw the police cars."

Ben thought he saw some of it splashed down the front of the guy, as well.

Interesting story but awfully convenient. People broke into the bank at the exact moment the boss was out? It raised a red flag. From Connor's frown, Ben realized he was not alone in wanting to dig around more in Kent's story.

"Everybody is fine." Connor's voice wasn't much better than the skeptical look on his face.

Joel pointed at the body bags. "Except for them."

"Who are they?" Kent asked without looking.

It was the one question Ben knew the answer to, so he handled it. "The bad guys."

Chapter Eleven

With his sleeves rolled up and his hair showing the tracks of his fingers, Connor stood at the head of the conference-room table on the first floor of the Corcoran Team headquarters later that night and looked around the room. "Let's run this."

Jocelyn heard the phrase but was too busy keeping her head from falling and smacking against the table to get all excited about being included in an information session. The adrenaline kick had long worn off. Now she had the afterburn of exhaustion. But no way was she leaving the room.

The entire building fascinated her. On the outside it looked like any other historically protected brick town house in this part of the city. Stately and expensive. But the inside had been carved up into something very different.

The big country kitchen with the blue cabinets at the back of the house fit. The front double rooms filled with computers and files and a conference area straight out of a spy movie looked more like a war room than a place for the family hangout.

This was where the real work happened. The behind-the-scenes gritty digging for leads. On the monitors stationed around the room and behind the security system complete with handprint identification and key cards.

They'd given her a seat at the table and she was going to sit in it, even if she almost fell asleep doing it.

A tray with a coffeepot and clean mugs sat on the middle of the table. Joel slid into the seat across from her and took a laptop out from where it was tucked under his armpit. Opening it, he looked up with his usual smile. "I'm ready."

"We need security footage, along with the name and all the information you can find about every business on that street."

Ben's voice, firm and angry, contrasted with the way he smoothed his hand up and down her thigh. Not sexual so much as soothing, yet the touch still made her want to crawl up onto his lap.

She tried to concentrate on what was being said and add in her concerns. "And where does the door from the upstairs balcony at the bank go?"

"Good question." Ben nodded. "Look into the blueprints, then check out the bank president, Kent Beane, and the security guy."

"Ed?" She thought about the older man who always greeted her with a smile. He made it a point to know people's names and open doors.

Seeing Ed as part of some grand conspiracy struck her as a waste of time. And a little scary. If the bad guys could get that close to her without her knowing, nowhere was safe.

"He disappeared for the entire robbery." Ben's fingers curled around the inside of her knee in a gentle squeeze.

An unexpected heat swirled through her. Okay, maybe she wasn't so tired after all. "Not to point out the obvious but Ed did shoot one of the attackers."

"You're both right." Joel waved a hand in the air without taking his attention from the computer screen. "I'll track this Ed guy on the tape and we'll see where he went. Could be a case of nerves. You know, a hiding-in-the-closet sort of thing. Some folks can't handle pressure."

She didn't like that explanation any more than the other one. "How comforting."

"I have a list of suggestions from Davis and Pax." Connor shot a file across the table in Joel's direction.

"Suggestions?"

"Davis used a different word but I'm trying to be tactful."

Joel laughed. "Must be killing them not to be in on this hard-core."

"Davis needs to stay where he is. By now whoever is coming after Jocelyn has to know something about our team, since we keep showing up next to the dead bodies. That means Kelsey and Lara need to stay in a protected space, just to be safe." There was nothing light in Ben's voice. The words settled in Jocelyn's mind. She hated every one of them. Ben was right but the underlying reality stung. She'd brought all this danger to their doors. Her, not Ben and not his team.

The guilt and worry balled up inside her. These men knew how to protect but her being there could cost them everything they cared about. She tried to think of another place she could go hide but nothing came to her.

Maybe some space and an hour or two to think would help. "As fun as this is, I need a break from the terror and attempted kidnappings and neverending need to throw up. I'm heading upstairs."

They all stared at her but Ben spoke up. "You okay?"

Clearly her voice had given her away. Either that or in her need for sleep she'd said something she only meant to think. "Not really."

Ben's arm slipped along the back of her chair and his fingers massaged her neck. The slow circle eased the thumping headache and kick-started a twirling in her stomach.

Some of the fatigue seeped out of her body and a new sensation set in. It looked as though her fear of gun-toting, commanding, strong men might be gone thanks to Ben.

On the list of everything about him that made her smile she added his tendency for public displays of affection. He had no trouble showing he cared for her in front of his friends. He didn't embarrass her or violate her privacy. She couldn't help but sink into the intimate way he touched her, as if it was something as matter-of-fact and normal as drinking coffee.

"You did great today," he said.

His automatic support was pretty great, too. From him that meant a lot, but she wasn't exactly ready to collect a medal for bravery. "I was plastered against the floor hoping not to get killed."

Joel smiled at her over the top of the laptop. "You stayed calm and called the warning that likely saved Ben's life."

"Damn," Ben groaned. "I meant to tell you not to share that yet."

All exhaustion vanished as she sat up straight. "What?"

"The trajectory of the hit on the attacker next to Ben suggested the bullet was aimed right at Ben's..." Joel froze in the process of turning the computer around to show her whatever was on his screen and stared at Ben instead. "What?"

Ben slipped his hand under her hair and turned her face toward him. "I'm fine. Thanks to you."

No, no, no. She had almost sat there and watched him get shot, all for her annoying habits and need to have repetition and uniformity.

She almost doubled over. "Now I am going up to vomit."

"You're fine."

"Don't bet on it." She had to get out of there. Find a quiet minute alone. So much had happened and she hadn't found two seconds to process it all.

She stood up, planning to find a shower and maybe sit on the bathroom floor by the toilet for a few minutes just in case. "I'm thinking it's inevitable at this point."

Ben winced. "In that case I might wait a while before I head up to join you."

Something about the big strong man being afraid of a woman getting sick made her laugh. "Chicken."

Because she couldn't resist, she brushed her fingers through his soft hair as she walked by. She wanted to lean down and kiss him, but that could be too much. With the world spinning and someone trying to grab her every two seconds, they hadn't exactly had a moment to sit down and talk about a definition for their relationship…if that was what it was.

He struck her as rock-solid, but kissing him in front of the guys could be the move that finally made him go all anti-commitment-male crazy. She just couldn't handle that loss on top of everything else.

"Hey, what was the teller's name?" Ben asked her as she reached the doorway to the main hall.

"What are you talking about?" Jocelyn gripped the doorjamb as she turned around. "Oh, you mean Pamela?"

Connor's eyebrow lifted. "Last name?"

Jocelyn was still stuck on the last question. "You think she has something to do with this?"

"She's the teller you go to regularly. You see her, she disappears and during the same time frame your life goes haywire. Seems too convenient not to be suspect," Joel explained as he typed away.

Ben glared at him. "*Disappeared* might be a strong word," he pointed out.

Jocelyn's head had taken off in a full spin now.

"Don't worry," Ben said. "We'll find out."

As Jocelyn walked up the steps, she thought of all the things she wasn't supposed to worry about. Her emotional baggage just got heavier with each passing second.

BEN FELT THE SENSATION of being stared at and decided not to lift his head and face whatever bugged Connor. Studying the file of Davis's notes provided cover. Not that Ben could read it. He stared at the words and lines of blue blur. All he could think about was the woman upstairs who could even now be stripping off her clothes and getting into a shower.

His control shattered.

"What about you? You okay?" Connor asked, clearly refusing to be ignored.

"Sure."

"I meant the gunfire."

The amusement in Connor's voice had Ben lifting his head. The flat line on the boss's mouth didn't match the tone. Concern played there, too. In his eyes, in the way he leaned forward. This wasn't about Jocelyn. It was about injuries, and Ben figured he could handle that talk.

"Can't lie. That was a close one. I felt the bullet whiz by my head." He knew it sounded nuts, but he could see the thing move through the air. That shot had come close to ending it all.

His bulletproof vest wouldn't have stopped the bullet to the head he'd only barely sidestepped. "I thought that was it."

"You're taking a lot of knocks on this case. Still think you should head to the hospital to take care of that filleting of your stomach," Joel said.

"Lucky for you Jocelyn has the skills to keep you mobile."

Connor nodded. "She's a good woman."

Ah, there it was. Didn't take Connor long to circle from gunfire to Jocelyn.

Ben cursed the ease with which he got sucked in. "Agreed, but why do I think I'm about to get a lecture about women and safety and how those things don't easily square with our work?"

Leaning back in his chair, Connor tapped his pen against his open palm. "She's got a lot of secrets."

"Don't we all?" The list went on for pages—the real story about the whereabouts of Connor's wife, everything about Joel's past and Ben's doubts about whether he had done the right thing in the NCIS case. And those were just the ones that came to him on the spot. Davis and Pax came from a family that defined dysfunctional. No one walked away clean on this one.

"You still have secrets?" Joel asked. "I'm thinking most of your life is on display right now."

Leave it to Joel to drill down to the point. He wasn't the type to tiptoe around anything, no matter how uncomfortable. The straight shooting tended to take the squirming out of most issues. This time Ben didn't mind. "Unfortunately, true."

"Just tread carefully with her." The intensity of Connor's voice suggested he wasn't kidding.

Even Joel glanced over at him. "You think she's a danger?"

"I think she's *in* danger and I'm guessing this isn't the first time." Connor's pen kept tapping. "But I think Ben knows that."

He knew most of the information but not all. That didn't stop him from wanting to go after the guy who terrified Jocelyn. Maybe he wouldn't jump in a car and drive to whatever prison the guy was in, but he could poke around and make sure the guy wasn't coming out anytime soon.

"There's a piece of crap who wouldn't take no for an answer from her and is now locked away." Ben stopped there. Jocelyn could fill in the rest if she wanted to.

Joel's jaw clenched. "Give me the name and I'll check in and make sure he's not instigating the attacks on her now. I'll refrain from arranging for him to get shanked in the group shower. Probably."

Connor nodded. "Focus on the check in part."

"Appreciate that." Ben knew they'd been outraged at the idea of some moron hurting Jocelyn or any other woman. Still, hearing the anger in their voices and seeing it in the way their shoulders tensed backed up what Ben already knew—regardless of how he'd ended up at Corcoran, he was in the right place.

The pen flipped fast enough for Connor to

launch it across the room. "You've had a rough few months, so be careful."

"Are you giving him the rebound speech?"

For some reason Joel's words made Ben smile. "Good question."

"I'm saying the timing of a relationship with her is not ideal."

Joel snorted. "Connor means it stinks."

Ben thought the same thing at least ten times a day. "You're not wrong about that."

"But I'm thinking you're going to keep seeing her." Connor didn't ask it as a question.

"Yeah, Connor. That is definitely going to happen."

SHE SHOULD HAVE gone back to her room.

She went to his.

Jocelyn stood in front of the dresser and ran her fingers over the folded stack of T-shirts and thought about how they fit over Ben's warm skin. One, two…she pulled out the third and frowned at the way one sleeve stuck out of the side. Before she could stop, she refolded it. Tucked the edges in just so. Switched the order, top to bottom, from light to dark.

The constant movement of her hands soothed her. Fixing things *just so* eased the anxiety that pinged around inside her. She'd endangered people, set off a chain of events that left people dead, and she had no idea how. The not knowing had her fought-for confidence puddling on the floor.

"Got twitchy when I couldn't find you." Ben leaned against the doorjamb watching her.

The idea he went hunting made her heart go a little wild. "Were you afraid I left the building? Because I'm not even sure that's possible."

"I was more worried I'd get stuck sleeping alone." He stepped into the room and stood next to her, facing the mirror above the dresser. "For the record, that would be a very bad thing."

"Tragic even."

"I agree." He folded his hand over hers and wove their fingers together. "How are you really doing?"

"My crazy is showing."

"The shirts?" He flipped through them with his other hand. "You can touch my clothes, my stuff—me—anytime."

"This sort of thing doesn't scare you?"

"Having someone try to kidnap you scares me." He lifted their clasped hands and kissed the back of hers. "Watching you overcome what haunts you fills me with nothing but awe. You impress the hell out of me."

Sweet-talking hottie.

He let go of her hand and his palm went to the side of her face. "Does the organizing help?"

"Still shaky." But the touching had her mind

switching gears to much more interesting topics. Being close to him, smelling him, watching him, it all calmed her nerves.

"I'd be worried if you were fine with all of this."

She could take anything. She'd learned that a year ago. She survived. But… "You almost died."

She clamped her mouth shut to keep the strangled sob from escaping her throat. Every time she closed her eyes, she saw him sliding across the floor. If he'd been hit, if she'd seen him go down… A dark, suffocating curtain fell over her at the thought.

She didn't know when or how he'd come to matter so much, but he had. Even when she'd pushed him away and given him every reason to move on to any of the other fifteen nurses who eyed him up, he'd never given up on getting to know her. He'd never gone for someone who might be easier to win over. And now he refused to walk away when any smart man would.

He turned her until they stood face-to-face and his hands massaged her upper arms. "I could have gotten hit, but I didn't. Focus on the latter."

The strength. She had no idea where he found it. He kept calling up reserves and never swayed. She envied that even keel.

But truth was he'd been sliced and shot and now almost killed because of her. "How can you look at it that way? Just shrug it off like the danger almost doesn't matter?"

"There isn't another way to move on."

She didn't wait for him to draw her close. She stepped into the circle of his arms and rested her hands against his muscled chest. "You got lucky and you wouldn't have needed to if I hadn't insisted on going to the bank."

"Whoa, back up." His fingers threaded through her hair and tipped her head back as his gaze searched her face. "Don't take that on."

"It was my fault and—"

A lingering kiss stopped her sentence. "I agreed you should go to the bank. Connor and Joel agreed. We own that blame."

"Because I insisted." His smile caught her off guard. "What?"

"Don't get all feisty on me when I say this, but we wouldn't have gone if I didn't want to."

"Because you're such a big, tough macho man." She snorted as she said it to let him know she wasn't buying the he-man act. "Oh, please."

"Do you forget I carry a gun?"

"Never." Seeing it used to touch off a strangling panic. Now, knowing he controlled his anger and could handle his weapon, never turning it on her, she felt nothing but safe.

"While I admit I am no match for you when

you pile on the charm and insist on getting your own way—"

Okay, now, that was ridiculous. She laughed. "When has that ever happened between us?"

"Even you could not topple the joint pressure of me, Connor and Joel." Ben's firm tone never wavered.

"You're saying you could have said no to me today?" That was not the way she remembered the conversation.

"I'm saying we're all grown-ups. The visit should have been fine and the fact it wasn't is one more piece of the puzzle."

Relief tumbled through her, erasing all those rough edges of guilt. She dropped her forehead to his impressive shoulder. "Dealing with this is so exhausting, and that's coming from a woman who is used to working brutal twelve-hour shifts on her feet."

"Hmm." That husky voice vibrated against her ear.

"What?" When she lifted her head again, she faced the bed and found her back balanced against the dresser. She didn't even remember moving.

His fingers traced the dip of the neckline of her T-shirt, skimmed over her collarbone and down to the tip of the shadow between her breasts. "I was kind of hoping you weren't tired."

Yeah, well, she was wide-awake now. "Subtle."

With a small tug, he lowered the shirt and slipped his thumb underneath. "I'm not sure I was trying to be."

His finger stroked over her nipple, making her gasp. "I bet I can be persuaded on this point."

"Oh, I will try very hard to convince you." Then he dropped his head and licked his tongue over the straining top of her breast. "Put every ounce of my energy into the task."

She forgot about guilt and fear. She forgot about everything but him.

Her hand went to the back of his head and she held him close. "Yes."

"We're never going to make it to the bed."

She didn't think they'd make it to the floor.

Chapter Twelve

Gary sat with his elbows balanced on the desk and his fingers steepled in front of his mouth. All of his focus stayed on the man across from him. The same one fidgeting as if he would jump out of his skin at any minute. Colin shifted and tugged on his pants. Even glanced around. None of it broke Gary's concentration.

They'd been back in the office for hours. The sun dipped and the night fell, and still they reviewed today's disastrous plan. The outcome cried out for punishment, but Gary refused to end Colin's torture that easily by killing him.

Gary sat and waited. He glanced at the clock on the wall and calculated the time since he last spoke.

Eleven minutes.

Colin crossed and uncrossed his legs, sending the chair into a symphony of creaking. When he opened his mouth, Gary broke in first. "I'm starting to believe Ms. Raine has some sort of power over men. Makes them stupid and sloppy."

"She brought the entire Corcoran Team to the bank with her."

"Not quite."

Gary had done his homework, or tried to at least. Finding information on the team had proved difficult. They had no website, and the internet appeared to be scrubbed clean of any reference to the business being involved in any project anywhere. He could find only a general reference to the general work they did.

Yet, their doors remained open, which meant paying clients. The leader's name, Connor, showed up now and then with veiled references about corporate risk assessments but without any real definition of what that meant.

The only clue was Ben Tanner. There was a name even the best hacker could not make disappear. Turned on his boss, took down the upper levels of NCIS. Yes, Ben had been a busy boy and now he'd appointed himself Jocelyn Raine's protector.

It wouldn't be hard to make him disappear and shift the blame to any number of disgruntled military types. Gary smiled at the thought. Tanner was the type of man who could experience an accident and no one would be surprised. Media coverage would likely include a "what did he expect would happen?" quote from anonymous sources. The fingers would point in a lot of directions, but not in Gary's, and the police would quietly close the case because that was what they did with snitches.

"No one expected a gun battle today. It was a simple snatch job. The men were to make it look like a robbery gone bad without being obvious about taking one woman," Colin said.

Gary saw the comments as further proof of his employee's incompetence. "You should have known this could go sideways. I did and I warned you. The men protecting her are not amateurs."

"And neither were the ones I hired."

"Your mistake was in thinking you would be able to control the situation when your dealings with this woman suggest anything but."

"You think the Corcoran Team knows about the data-and-funds exchange?"

There was no other explanation. They protected for a living and they were currently protecting her. Had been from that first night at her apartment.

Protecting her meant making his life difficult, and Gary was just about done with that nonsense. "It's beginning to look that way."

"What about Detective Willoughby? He's on every crime scene."

Gary lowered his hands to the desk. "I'm not worried about him."

"Really?"

Colin refused to learn. The last thing Gary wanted was a challenge to his authority. When Colin paid for his failures in this matter, Gary would lead with that one.

"My main concern now is blowback. Being implicated," he said, ignoring the question that started a tic in his jaw. "I need to know what can be traced to me, which means I need to know what Corcoran knows."

Right now he'd be happy to know *what* exactly Corcoran was.

"You going to plant a device in their head-quarters?" Colin asked as his jumping around subsided.

Normally that would resolve the issue. Gary would devise a way in, have his best people set up the equipment and collect the data. But that didn't work with a company like Corcoran that thrived on playing the clandestine card. "I assume they'd find it, and that's under the assumption I could even get past whatever security they have and get it in there."

"Understood."

Gary doubted that. "No, I think there's only one way to get this done in the time we have left."

"How?"

Gary no longer had a choice. "I'm going to walk through the front door."

"What?"

"Better yet, I'm going to bring them to me. Tomorrow morning."

BEN COULDN'T SHAKE the tickling sensation at the base of his neck. The two-story drapes were drawn, blocking out the sun and the view to the street beyond. The bank stayed closed, which was a problem, since this was a local bank with few branches. The locked doors and police tape kept people out.

Being in this cavernous room the day after the attack explained part of his unease. Standing next to the counter in the middle of the room where he almost bit it didn't help. Neither did watching Jocelyn page through the deposit slips that once fanned over the top but now were stacked in neat piles.

She shuffled them, then straightened them again. The repetitive action seemed to soothe her. The neater the pile, the less her hands shook. That she'd figured out a way to quiet the demons inside her left him humbled. He knew how the noises and doubts could grow into a deafening thunder, but she kept them at bay. It just made him gut-sick that she had to.

He reached over and touched his fingertips to

hers. Nothing too obvious. Not with Ed and Joel circling the balcony upstairs for clues and Connor questioning Kent at a desk a few feet away.

They were sleeping together and Ben wasn't about to hide it or lie about it. Kissing her at the conference-room table this morning with Joel and Connor watching probably ended any questions on that score. But he could hold off on a general broadcast of his preferred sleeping arrangements until they had the "we're exclusive now" talk, and he definitely planned on having that soon.

He waited until she glanced up. The wary darkness in her eyes had vanished somewhat, but not totally. "You okay being here?" he asked.

She looked over and around, taking in every inch of the first floor before answering. "I see the shooting when I close my eyes. It hardly matters if I'm here or back at the house."

Not that he could blame her. The latest shootout was on a slow-motion reel in his head, as well. "For a few hours last night, you seemed to forget."

She slipped her fingers through his. "And I plan to use that tactic again tonight."

"Never been called a tactic before." This woman could call him anything she wanted. Could do anything she wanted with him. They'd been on fast-forward since they met and he did not want to slow them down.

Joel broke the spell when he walked up beside

her. His gaze stopped on their joined hands but he didn't say anything. Still, hand-holding at a crime scene qualified as unprofessional and borderline stupid, so Ben gave the back of her hand a quick rub and then let go.

"Anything upstairs?" he asked Joel.

"An old balcony. Ed says there used to be a second floor, and the architect who did the redesign put the balcony in for aesthetics and some sort of ode to the place's former glory." Joel pointed out the walkway above them as he talked. "We went up and the only way out is through an emergency door to the roof and then down a ladder to the outside."

Jocelyn grabbed the closest stack of deposit slips and tapped them on the table, lining up the edges with precision. "So, the robbers just went up there for a walk? Doesn't make sense."

"I think we've established they weren't robbing anything." Joel watched her but again had the good sense to stay quiet.

Ben hadn't shared the compulsive behaviors. He probably didn't have to. Joel had helped him check her bedroom that first night. Clothing lined up with the exact amount of space between each hanger. The color coding. The perfect edge where she lined up her shoes.

Having been in the military, Ben recognized the symptoms of post-traumatic stress disorder.

She never used the term. He doubted she'd been diagnosed. She talked about behavioral adjustments. More than likely, she handled the whole thing herself.

"Let me ask this." Jocelyn had them both staring at her now. "If this wasn't about taking money or things out of safe deposit boxes, then why didn't they just grab me and run?"

There was only one answer to that, so Ben gave it to her. "Because they had to make it look like a robbery."

"That guy seem okay to you?" Joel leaned against the table and nodded in Kent's direction.

The man sat at his desk in full-on fidget mode. Sweat dotted his brow and he kept wiping his hand over his mouth.

Ben had noticed the nervous tics before. They struck him as even more pronounced today, which made no sense at all. The danger had passed. He should be celebrating living through it or at least look more relaxed.

"To be fair, his bank was robbed, kind of," Jocelyn said.

Joel nodded. "While he was out."

There was a clicking sound as Jocelyn tapped the pile of slips against the table. "Still thinking it's too convenient?"

"Connor will break him." Even now Ben admired Connor's work. He kept his voice low and his gestures smooth as Kent unraveled into a bucket of sweat.

"No question."

Ben turned around to agree with Joel and saw Ed usher a man in the front door of the bank. "Hey, you can't be in here."

That was the deal. They had all come to get the search done faster. That meant bringing Jocelyn outside the house again, and Ben had laid down a bunch of rules to make sure that happened. Being in the bank with only Ed and Kent was one of them.

The new guest walked right over, just a few steps behind Jocelyn. Joel moved to block the direct line to her and Connor came up out of his chair with his hand on his gun. Ben beat them both. Ignoring the pull of the stitches across his stomach and the tightness over his shoulder, he vaulted around the table and put his body right in front of hers.

"Not one more step." And he would put a bullet in the guy to back up his threat if he had to.

Forget the expensive black suit and successful-businessman trappings. The guy was forty-something and fit and could be a killer for all Ben knew. He wasn't about to play wait-and-see on that one.

The man's eyebrow lifted. "Since my money is

in this bank, I believe I can do whatever I think is appropriate."

Connor shook his head as he walked over and through the wall of tension. "Sir, you have to—"

"It's okay." Kent rushed in with his hands in the air. Nervous energy radiated off him as he flailed. "This is Gary Taub."

Gary stood in direct contrast to the bank manager. A good five inches taller and totally put together. He frowned when he saw the sweat pouring off Kent, then dismissed him by turning to Connor. "I own the building next door."

"I'm guessing you don't mean the coffee shop," Joel said.

Gary didn't break eye contact with Connor. It was as if he knew who was in charge and refused to deal with anyone he deemed lower on the food chain. "Worldwide Securities."

"What kind of business is that?"

"Financial."

"What can we do for you, Mr. Taub?" Connor shifted away from the group and took the spotlight off the place where Jocelyn stood.

She hadn't said a word. She was too busy digging her nails into Ben's back.

"Gary, please." The man almost bowed as he said it. "I'm checking on Kent."

That made almost no sense in Ben's mind. If Kent weren't a complete mess, maybe. As it was, Ben couldn't imagine Gary hanging out with schlubby, balding Kent unless Gary needed something from him. Gary just seemed that type.

"Are you two business associates?" Ben asked.

"We share an interest in keeping the area safe." Gary's gaze finally landed on Ben. Did a quick flick over his shoulder to Jocelyn, then back again. "And you are?"

"Connor Bowen," he said before Ben could answer. "This is my team."

"Of what?"

"Investigators."

The corner of Gary's mouth eased up. "For the police?"

"Maybe we could ask you a few questions."

Gary folded his hands in front of him. "I notice you're not answering any."

"That's how this game is played."

A terse silence followed the verbal volleying. If this Gary guy wanted a battle, Connor was not the right guy to pick as an adversary. Connor didn't blink. Didn't call any attention to the rest of the team, which was good because if Ben guessed correctly, Joel was using that fancy phone, held low in his hand, to get a photo of Gary.

Gary finally broke the quiet with a quick nod. "Well, I can tell you what I saw on the day of the incident."

"You were here?" Ben ran through his mental roll call of faces from that day and knew this guy was not on it.

"Next door."

Connor stepped back and gestured in the general direction of Kent's abandoned desk chair. "Then have a seat."

Everyone pivoted. Ed took up his old position at the door while Connor sat with Gary and ran him through a series of questions as Kent watched. No, while Kent stared at the large clock on the wall by the safe. The guy didn't sit still. Gary must have noticed because more than once he glanced up and scowled at his supposed business friend.

It took Ben a second to realize he stood alone. He spun around and found Jocelyn back at the counter in the middle of the room with Joel hovering over her shoulder like the bodyguard he was.

Ben walked back to her. He was about to make a joke but he noticed her hands. She'd stopped straightening. She turned the slips over and studied the back.

He knew something ran through her mind. "What's wrong?"

"Something."

He balanced his palms against the edge of the table and leaned in, keeping his voice at a whisper level. "Can you be a little more specific?"

"The deposit slips."

He still wasn't getting it. "One more detail might help."

"What about them?" Joel asked.

"No one gave me anything except Pamela." Jocelyn held up a slip.

From what Ben could see, it was blank except for the preprinted blocks. "What are we talking about?"

"The first attacker talked about me having something." The slip flapped when Jocelyn shook it.

Ben remembered the question the first attacker had asked her. They'd all turned it over many times. The team took turns asking her about it, trying to get to the heart of it. Was it something from a patient or doctor that the guy was after? But none of their questions had gone anywhere. "I thought we decided that was some sort of line to throw you off."

"The last time I saw Pamela, I did some banking and she gave me the receipts. She put them in an envelope, just like she always did." Jocelyn smiled. "Don't you see what I'm saying? *She* handed me something."

"And now she's missing." It didn't take long to put two and two together and figure out Pamela was dead. When Jocelyn kept talking, Ben knew she hadn't made that leap yet.

"I forgot because it was so mundane, and I assumed the attacker was talking about something that happened at the hospital." Jocelyn's voice rose as she talked.

Joel answered her in a whisper. "I'm thinking we can now assume Pamela is dead."

The color ran right out of Jocelyn's cheeks. She morphed from excited to pale in a second.

Ben hated the look of defeat he saw on her face. "Joel."

"Being realistic here." He shrugged.

Jocelyn waved her hand in front of her face. "It's okay. I need to know."

"But do you have any clue where you threw this slip or whatever it was away?" Joel blew out a long breath. "I mean, the chances of finding it are...what?"

"No." Ben kept shaking his head. "She didn't throw it away."

"I have it," she confirmed.

It took Joel a few more steps to catch up. "At your apartment?"

Still ghostly-white, Jocelyn managed to smile. "At Corcoran."

GARY STOOD AT the front door, just inside the bank, and watched the Corcoran Team rush out of there. After a tap on his shoulder from Ben, Connor had listened and then hustled them all out of there.

The man asked one wrap-up question and they were gone.

Kent rocked back on his heels. "They didn't act like they knew you. I don't think—"

"You shouldn't because you'd be wrong." Kent didn't see it, but Gary did.

Kent frowned. "What?"

"Up until five minutes ago, she didn't know she had the note." From a few feet away, Gary had watched the realization dawn on her face. She went from mindlessly playing with the papers to holding one up. Her excitement spilled over until one of the men said something and then they mobilized.

She knew. In a few minutes, they would all know. Gary couldn't control what was in the note from the teller, but he could get his hands on it.

"How do you know what she knew and when?" Kent asked.

Gary didn't feel inclined to explain to a man who wouldn't survive until morning. "The look on the woman's face and the way they ran out of here."

"The transfer is in a few hours." Kent looked around but Ed was on the other side of the room. "You promised to let my wife go."

Whether he promised or not didn't matter because Gary had no intention of letting that happen. Neither did his silent partner, since Sharon had most definitely seen his partner's face when he grabbed her. That made her collateral damage.

Yes, the Beane family would not survive the night. They'd die and the attempted bank robbery would be linked back to Kent as an operation gone wrong. Sharon as the innocent victim unaware of her husband's money issues and schemes. In Gary's scenario, Sharon found out, a fight ensued and the resulting murder-suicide would stand as one more horrific tale of a marriage on the edge and a desperate man who took a terrible turn.

At least that was where the evidence Gary manufactured would lead the police to believe.

"I have a very small window in which to fix your mess," he said to the man who would provide access then soon be dead.

"I didn't—"

"Stop." Baiting this man proved quite enjoyable. "For Sharon's sake, you better hope I can do it."

Chapter Thirteen

Jocelyn drew the envelope out of her purse and put it on the Corcoran conference-room table on top of the files and papers and everything else they had thrown all over the place. She beat back the urge to organize it all. This wasn't their first job and they knew how to do their work, but still.

Joel grabbed the envelope as soon as it hit the table. "You kept a receipt from more than a week ago?"

"I keep everything." She snatched it back and waved it in front of him from across the table. "Sometimes being a woman on the edge helps."

Joel frowned. "Excuse me?"

She turned to Ben at his position next to Connor at the end of the table. For some reason she wanted Ben to be the one to see it first. "Here."

"In your purse." Ben shook his head. "No wonder the guy couldn't find it at the house. Also makes sense we missed it. I'd never think to tell a woman to dump her purse. Seems like a sure-fire way to get my butt kicked."

"We will from now on," Joel said.

Connor rested his hands on the back of her chair. "I'm not sure I knew she had it here."

"I keep receipts in my purse and reconcile every Friday. I was attacked before I could." It sounded crazy when she said it out loud.

Never mind how smooth and perfect they fit together and how she had them lined up inside the envelope with not one edge sticking out. Just when she thought she'd come so far, she ran smack into evidence she had some work to do.

Ben shot her one of his sexy smiles. "I love your need for order."

One look at that mouth and her bones melted. After living with the anxiety as a curse for so long, she had her first moment of clarity. Maybe this one time he was right and it saved her. "Right now I do, too."

She glanced down at the words on the paper. The last two stood out to her as if they were set off in flashing lights.

Worldwide Securities transfer. Sharon kidnapped.

He read the words and Jocelyn jumped in with the first question. "Who is Sharon?"

"Kent's wife." Joel sat down and started typing. "Let's see where she is."

Jocelyn glanced at Ben. "More kidnappings."

"Yeah, I know." The sadness in his eyes translated to a vibration of anger in his voice.

After a series of ultrafast clicking, Joel made a noise. "Hmm, not good."

"What?" Connor asked.

"A teacher who, from what I can see here, is out on unexpected temporary leave. Kent said she's very ill."

"Funny how he forgot to mention that fact." Ben blew out a long breath. "Guess her being gone explains his constant sweating."

That made three women—Pamela, this Sharon and her. Jocelyn's chest ached at the thought she might be the only safe one. "So, someone is planning to take money from the bank? I still don't get it. They were in the bank and didn't steal anything."

"It all comes down to Gary Taub, owner of Worldwide and our sudden visitor this afternoon," Ben said.

Joel kept typing. "Thought that seemed a bit too smooth."

"So did he."

Ben's dislike for the guy had been immediate. He didn't exactly hide his feelings, with all that grumbling at the bank. Jocelyn had chalked it up to his protective instincts and having someone break through their security barrier thanks to Ed. Now she wondered if Ben's anger went deeper. The instant hate could have something to do with his innate ability to sense danger.

If so, she wanted to know. "What was this Gary guy doing? Why walk in and risk giving himself away?"

Ben shrugged. "More than likely checking us out."

"Then we should be fine." One business guy against all of them. Add in Pax and Davis, and Jocelyn tried to imagine how quickly Gary would go down. Then she noticed the three of the guys in question staring at her...waiting. "Oh, come on. This team is scary. What sane person would take you all on?"

Joel burst out laughing. "Thank you, I think."

"Let's go through the blueprints, construction grids, anything that could connect these two buildings in physical ways." The usual stern thread moved through Connor's voice but the look on his face came off suspiciously like a smile. "Anything on the bank security tapes?"

Joel shook his head. "All wiped clean. The most recent is from three weeks ago."

"What did Ed and Kent say about that?" Ben said as he took the seat next to her.

"They can't explain it."

In a few moves, they all shifted into their regular chairs, her next to Ben and Connor at the head. It was so natural that she wondered if they secretly practiced the maneuver.

With the head seat came the power, and Connor immediately stepped into the role. "Maybe this Gary person can."

"You think he's planning a bank robbery?" she asked, because she still couldn't wrap her head around the attacks being separate from the pile of money that sat in the bank safe.

"He's next door to the bank, which appears to be the epicenter of whatever's happening there." Ben punctuated each word with a thump of his finger against the table. "I'm willing to bet that balcony leads to Worldwide somehow."

Joel paged through the papers and flipped the blueprints out and on top. "Not that I could see."

"What do we know about him or the company?" Ben asked Joel.

"Wealthy financial guy. High-end brokerage. Lost his wife to cancer and a brother in a freak accident overseas. There's no one else as far as I can tell."

"So, we've got a guy with nothing to lose. That's the worst kind." Connor snatched a folder off the desk behind him and opened it. "We missed something. I want it found in the next thirty minutes. Call Davis and Pax and get them in on this by video conference."

Ben was too busy swearing under his breath to look at anything. "Fine, but in thirty-one minutes I'm taking Jocelyn to the garage."

"Sounds dirty," Joel said without lifting his head from the blueprint study.

As if they had an extra few minutes to check out a car. But when no one explained, Jocelyn went searching for one. "Uh, why?"

Ben's head came around and he stared at her. "Gun practice."

The intense look shot right through her. His mood shifted to serious and the heat in his eyes told her not to argue. This wasn't sexual, as Joel joked. This was more like an order. For the first in a long time, the tone didn't make her throw up a solid emotional wall in defense.

"We're going to shoot cars?" she asked when he didn't cough up another answer. Leave it to Ben to go quiet all of a sudden, just when she needed more information.

"It's not really a garage."

Again he stopped and again she had to poke him until he said something helpful. "What is it?"

"A weapons depot of sorts—and you're not going to shoot. We'd need a range and we can't get to one without further endangering you. The plan is to work on aim, show you how the weapons work, get you comfortable holding one." Ben laid it all out, then leaned back in his chair.

It was as if he waited for her to scream or have a fit. She half expected those feelings to rush up on her, but they didn't. Anxiety bubbled inside her as it always did but the overwhelming need to flee didn't hit her. She chalked that up to progress.

Probably also had something to do with the emotional free fall she'd been in for more than a week. That had one source—Ben. He smiled, he frowned, he spoke to her in a quiet whisper or he clenched his jaw, like he was doing now, and her heart performed a happy little spin.

He'd gone from potential date to bodyguard and now to the man she wanted in her life. The change smacked into her as her breath whooshed out. This was more than a free fall—it was a falling-for-him kind of thing.

She shoved back from the table and almost put her head between her knees. Would have if she didn't have an audience.

When he frowned at her, she knew she wasn't hiding the realization all that well but suspected he thought she got nauseous at the idea of guns. Not at all. She got it now. Sometimes the good guys needed to be armed.

Right before he could say something, she collected her jangling nerves and forced out a question. "And why do I need these gun skills?"

Connor broke in. "He needs you to be ready."

Okay. That didn't answer anything. "For what?"

Ben's hand hit the back of her chair and he spun her so that she faced him. "Anything."

Two HOURS LATER Ben watched Jocelyn massage her palm with her opposite thumb. She'd followed every direction without arguing or passing out. When he first mentioned the guns, he thought she'd slide right under the conference-room table. Not now.

No way was he going to resist kissing her. Seemed wrong what with everything brewing around them and her obvious distress, but the need started backing up on him and he wanted a release.

"You're pretty amazing."

She glanced up at him. Her bright smile came a beat later. "You're not bad yourself."

He put the last of the guns in the locked cabinet and closed the false wall. When he leaned back against the workbench, she stepped right into the space between his legs. It was as if the woman was made for him.

He curled a piece of her soft auburn hair around his index finger. "Strong, beautiful, smart."

"You are a sweet-talking man." Her fingers fiddled with the buttons on his shirt. She unbuttoned the top one and traced the collar of the white T-shirt underneath.

If they weren't standing in the middle of a pile of weapons, he'd be stripping that sexy tank top off her right now. He settled for something more G-rated. "I'd rather be the man you're kissing."

Her hand slipped up his neck to the back of his head. "We can make that happen."

With a gentle pressure, she brought his head down. Not that it took much to get him going. The start of an erection pressed against his fly and air hammered in his lungs. There wasn't a moment he didn't want her.

A loud beep came right before Joel's voice broke into the heavy breathing. "How is it going?"

Ben's head dropped right before their lips met. He looked up and shot his teammate a death glare. "Apparently it's not going to happen this second."

Joel smiled as he looked from Ben to Jocelyn. "Did I interrupt something?"

"No," she said but she didn't jump back or out of his arms.

That was the only thing keeping him from lunging across the room and strangling Joel. "Yes."

She let her hands slide down Ben's chest. When she turned around to face Joel, Ben caught her with one finger hooked through her belt loop. He was fine with her staying close. Plus, she hid a bulge that Joel would give him crap about for days if he saw it.

"What's up?" she asked with the amusement still evident in her voice.

"A missing fourteen feet."

Maybe it was a sign of what was going on when Joel burst in, but Ben couldn't make sense of the comment. "Excuse me?"

"Checked the blueprints and compared to the photos I took inside the bank and the ones I have from outside on the street. Did a bunch of measurements—"

Ben smiled. "Of course you did."

"—and there's something between those two buildings, between the bank and Gary's place."

"Maybe the bank's safe." Jocelyn shifted as if she planned to step away.

With his hands on her hips, Ben pulled her back against him.

Joel shook his head. "No, this is on the second floor, above the safe."

The beeping returned. Only this wasn't one long squeal to signal the lock being disengaged. This was a motion detector.

She stiffened. "What is that?"

This time Ben let her pull away. The shot of adrenaline killed off the last of the sexual desire brewing inside him. It sputtered right out as he unlocked the cabinet behind him and grabbed the silencers and vests.

"We've got company," he said as he turned her around and put the Kevlar on her. Then he opened her palm and put a small gun in it. "Good thing you're a quick learner."

She stared at the weapon where it lay in her hand. "All this because someone's at the door of the house? Maybe just ratchet down the testosterone and tell whoever it is to go away."

Ben hadn't put up the garage windows. Metal shutters covered every entrance but the door. From the outside, they looked like part of the wall. Nothing out of the ordinary. From the inside, complete armored protection.

Joel reached under the cabinet at the far side of the four-berth garage and a monitor flashed on. Darkness had begun to fall but the security system found the heat signatures. The images adjusted, moving in click by click. The closest camera pinned them at the house's back porch.

"No cookie-selling there." Joel pointed at the man near the kitchen door. "This one? He's not visiting. That's a gun he's holding."

Jocelyn leaned in close and squinted at the screen. "More attackers. You've got to be kidding. Here?"

"Looks like we scared dear ol' Gary," Ben said and Joel nodded.

"What?" She seemed to be having some trouble taking it all in. She turned around in the open space as the familiar look of fear crossed her mouth and her eyes glazed. "You think he sent commandos."

"We meet him and suddenly we have people with guns stalking this place. Nobody followed us back here, so yeah, I blame Gary." Joel clipped on a shoulder holster and put his usual gun in it while he held the one with the silencer.

She shot him a "you've lost your mind" glare. "How do you know no one was behind us?"

"I know."

Ben decided to spare her the car speech from Joel. The man knew his vehicles and could maneuver through the streets with ease. He also had a sense when he was being followed and didn't think twice of circling around for hours to lose someone. "It's one of Joel's specialty areas. It would be hard for someone to tie this property to the team, but if you have skills and access to the right databases, it's not impossible."

"Connor might want to work on that." She pulled her cell out of her front jeans pocket. "On that topic, shouldn't we warn him there are two guys on his back porch?"

"Oh, he knows." No sooner had Ben made

the comment than a light in the house's kitchen went on.

"He's walking right into a trap." Jocelyn stepped forward.

Ben grabbed her by the back of the shirt. "You stay here."

"But Connor needs—"

Feeling her body tremble under his hands, Ben leaned down and whispered in her ear, "He's only opening that back door when he wants it open. He's got this. I promise."

As if they'd conjured him up, Connor's voice broke through the garage. Jocelyn jumped and let out a little squeal. Ben held a hand against her but joined Joel in watching that back door across the yard.

The intercom speaker was in the ceiling and Connor gave a play-by-play on the whole scene as it unfolded outside. That was what happened when you had a state-of-the-art security system.

"Two heat signatures. I'm coming around the side in five." Connor's steady voice echoed as he started the countdown. "Five…four…"

Jocelyn's eyes widened. "Is Connor crazy?"

"Popular question." Ben pointed at the far wall. "You stand there and don't move."

"I have a gun."

Now was not the time for this. Joel inched toward the door to the backyard and sent Ben the "move it" signal, so he went for the hard truth. "And I don't want to worry about you being shot."

"Okay."

That was almost too easy. "Like that?"

"This time, yes. Go." She went on tiptoes and gave him a quick kiss on the lips.

"Two…one…"

Forcing his head back in the game, Ben took his position on the opposite side of the doorway. He nodded at Joel as he slammed the garage door open and the humid night air rushed in. The two in the yard spun around at the sound. The one on the right didn't even get his gun aimed before Joel peeked around the doorway and nailed him in the shoulder. When he tried to get off an off-balance second shot, Ben's shot took him down.

The steady pings of gunfire rang out. The silencers filtered most of the noise, and the property's setback in a group of trees and up on a hill hid the rest. The one remaining attacker took a hit to the thigh and doubled over. His leg seemed to go to sleep. He dragged it behind him as he tried to take cover on the back porch. The railing didn't help and Connor didn't keep furniture there. It was an open space and gave the team an unrestricted shot.

Another shot and the guy went down. On his elbow and still shooting, he dragged his body to the back door. His shots went wide as the barrel bounced around from all the shifting. Nerves seemed to be settling in and his movements turned jerky.

Got him.

Ben gave Joel the signal to move outside. "Let's go."

They could disarm the guy and grab him for questioning. Crouched and going in, they ran across the backyard. The attacker did a double take at the wall of men coming at him. Going faster now, he groaned and half crawled toward the side of the house. His hand slapped against the wooden slats as his gun clanked at his side.

He made it a few feet, but only thanks to the lack of firepower coming at him because of the stated goal to take the guy alive. Joel and Ben were up on him, just a few feet behind, when Connor moved out of the shadows and stepped on his hand hard with a work boot.

"That's far enough."

The guy screamed as the crunching sound filled the night air.

"That had to—"

Joel's words were cut off as the attacker made a lunging move. A gun appeared in his other hand and a roar of rage escaped him as he aimed for Connor's stomach.

Ben slammed a bullet in the back of the attacker's head before he could fire the shot. He fell in a boneless, dead fall, thudding against the wood.

Connor dropped down on the balls of his feet and felt for a pulse. He picked up the weapons as he shook his head. "He's done."

Ben refused to feel sorry about that. He went off plan, but Connor's death wasn't on the menu, either.

Connor stood up and glanced over at Ben. "Thanks for that."

"You guys made that sort of gunfire runaround thing look easy." Jocelyn offered the comment as she started across the yard. She still held the gun. Instead of shaking on her feet, she walked tall and the tremble in her voice stayed at a minimum.

In that moment, Ben knew she'd ignored his order. She'd been outside and watched it all. She wasn't the type to hide. Not anymore.

That she walked into danger frustrated him, but he admired her spirit. Other people in her position, including many of the tough guys he worked with at NCIS, would be asking for protective custody and riding the danger out in a hotel somewhere. Not her.

Still, the urge to pack her off did kick strong. "You okay?"

She looked at all three Corcoran men but not

at the guys on the ground. "I had the safe part of the job. Just stood over there with my fingers ready to dial 9-1-1."

Connor put his hands on his hips. "I hate when people come to the house. You're just begging to be shot when you step on my property without an invitation."

"Obviously," she said. "So, now what?"

"We clear these two out." Velcro ripped as Connor grabbed his phone out of a pocket in his vest.

"How exactly?" Her question sounded more confused than anything.

Ben couldn't blame her. Until he threw in with Corcoran, he'd never known a private group who could "handle" this sort of thing. People broke in, you called the police.

Not Connor. He had government and police contacts, and depended on those to clean up a lot of messes. To preserve Corcoran's anonymity and ability to do the job, Connor kept the name out of reports and the paper. In exchange for letting other law-enforcement agencies get the credit, Corcoran stayed undercover.

"We know people," he said.

Jocelyn smiled at that. "You mean Detective Willoughby?"

His smile slipped at the mention of the new

guy Connor didn't have under control. "Not if I can help it."

"I guess that means it's time for me to finally throw up as I've been promising, then go to sleep with a gun under my pillow." She shot Ben a side-glance as she mentioned that last part.

He hated to postpone whatever she had in mind, but he knew Connor would want to move. You did not crash his house and expect him to wait to respond. "Connor plans for us to leave in the next ten minutes."

"Exactly," Connor said. "We call Kent and demand a meeting. I want us back in that bank right now. No more waiting, because the bad guys sure aren't."

"But they aren't winning," Ben pointed out because he wanted to put a lid on the anxiety welling inside him. "You know, to the extent that means anything."

"If I have to break through that wall on the bank's second story, we're seeing what's behind there. I'm tired of the lying and games."

Joel pocketed two more weapons from those scattered on the ground. "I can stay here with Jocelyn. Guard her or maybe take her over to Davis and Pax for safekeeping, then circle around to give you backup."

"We all go." Connor glanced around. "And we

need these bodies moved before a nosy neighbor decides to go for a walk and calls in the cavalry."

The words sent a shock of denial through Ben. Connor was the boss, but still... "All of us are going to the bank?"

Jocelyn nodded. "Except for the part where I've lost all feeling in my legs, I agree with that plan."

"You do?" Connor must have found it funny because her response eased some of the strain over his eyes.

"If the bad guys are storming the house, I'm not going to be here to welcome them. I would much rather be wherever you guys are." She frowned at Joel. "And what are you thinking? I am not leading attackers to a pregnant woman's front door, so forget about the Davis angle."

On one level—the professional, commonsense one—Ben knew that was the right answer. That didn't mean he liked it. His brain and body were definitely not working together on this plan "We'll see."

Joel joined Connor in smiling. "I'm thinking we're growing on Jocelyn here. She's started to get used to having us around."

"I think you're basically comparing us to mold," Connor pointed out.

She stepped over the first attacker and headed for the back porch. Her footing faltered when she looked down, but she quickly recovered. "Call yourselves whatever you want, but I'm coming along."

Ben knew she'd made up her mind. That meant he was stuck now.

Chapter Fourteen

They got to the bank across town in record time. Jocelyn stood in Kent's private office with a wall of male protection around her. Safe and cocooned by Corcoran Team members with Ben at her back and Connor and Joel on either side. But she couldn't shake the feeling that something was off. Really off.

Kent sat in his big leather chair and twirled his cell phone around in his fingers. Between the fidgeting and the sweat staining the armpits of his dark blue shirt, she almost felt sorry for him. Or she would if it weren't so obvious he was hiding something. Even Ed stood guard at his side, frowning down at him.

"Anything you want to say, Kent?" Connor asked for the second time, this version in a lower, huskier "I'm done with you" tone.

Jocelyn realized if he used that voice with her she might crawl under a desk. He sounded two seconds away from whipping that gun out and taking aim. Clearly the man did not like people storming his house.

Plastic thudded against the wooden desk as Kent dropped the phone, then slapped it flat against the top. "It is after hours. Why did you call me here?"

"Wrong question." Ben shifted his weight until his legs were hip-width apart and he crossed his arms over his chest. "We should be asking why you were already at the bank at this hour and not home with your wife."

"It is almost midnight," Joel added.

"My life is not your business." Kent slid the phone toward him under his palm.

Before the cell traveled one more inch, Ed reached over and snatched it. Jocelyn had been about to do the same thing and sent Ed a half smile in appreciation for stopping all the unnecessary banging.

Connor didn't move. "Oh, I think it is."

"Not to cause trouble, but what is going on here?" Ed asked. "It's late and the bank's business is done. Why not meet at Kent's house or at the police station? I don't understand."

"Because they're not police." Kent reached for the phone. "Maybe we should call and double-check their authority."

Connor shrugged. "Go ahead."

When Kent hesitated and the phone stayed

in the cradle, Jocelyn zeroed in on the subject that mattered most to her. "Call your wife while you're at it. I'd love to meet her."

"What?" Kent's gaze flew to Jocelyn's. "I barely know who you are."

Maybe it was the tone or the way his gaze met hers then quickly skidded away. A bunch of tiny little clues that led to one very obvious conclusion—he knew exactly who she was and not just because she used this branch for her banking.

No, guilt vibrated off him. He had put her in danger or he had stood back and let it happen. She'd bet her life on it, and that was exactly what she'd been doing for days, whether she knew it or not.

"I think you do." Jocelyn gained confidence the more the thought spun around in her mind. "You know who I am and why I'm in danger."

Ben put a hand against the small of her back. "She's the one your employee dragged into this mess. The one people keep trying to kidnap or kill."

After a swallow big enough to see his throat move, Kent folded his hands together on the desk in front of him. Then unfolded them. Then they disappeared on his lap. "I understand the bank robbery was upsetting, but—"

"Enough." Connor barked out the warning, and all motion and the small noises in the room stopped. Even the desk chair ceased creaking as Kent rocked.

"What?" he asked as he wiped away a new sheen of sweat on his forehead.

"Stop with whatever you're hiding." The words exploded out of Jocelyn. The frustration that had been building finally burst loose and she refused to hold off one more second from breaking into the interrogation. "Enough women are dead."

Kent's head wobbled as if he was about to go down. "What are you talking about?"

Ed stepped in closer, glancing from Kent to the rest of the room. "Wait, uh, who's dead?"

"Okay, this isn't getting us anywhere." Connor pointed at the ceiling. "Where does the staircase up to the balcony eventually lead?"

"Emergency exit." Ed gave the answer.

Connor ignored him. "Where else?"

Jocelyn liked his style. All of them, actually. She started thinking of them as her men. They came in, they took charge, they refused to back down and they were willing to die for women they didn't even know. Even now Ben touched her back, giving her a lifeline and reassuring her of his presence.

"We checked." Ed nodded in Joel's direction. "Right? There's nothing else up there."

Connor exhaled, letting his displeasure flow over the room. "That's not true, is it, Kent?"

"Keep in mind this is your last chance to come clean," Ben said from behind her.

Kent started shaking his head and didn't stop. "You can't do anything worse to me."

Joel took a step closer. "Worse than what?"

"Me."

At the sound of the familiar male voice, Jocelyn felt a hand push her forward and heard Ben yell at her to move. She stumbled into the desk and looked around in time to see Gary press a gun to the back of Ben's head.

Another man pointed one right at Connor's face. The surprise visitors had them all shifting and all weapons up and aimed.

She still hadn't processed all she was seeing when Kent stood up and his chair shot back. The men crowded closer to Ben's side of the desk until the guy with Gary pulled a second weapon and aimed that one, too.

Everyone had moved but Ben. He had picked pushing her out of the way and getting her out of the direct attack line over getting a jump on his attacker. He'd traded his body for hers.

Seeing him now, hands raised and anger straining in every muscle of his face, had her fighting off a gasp. She would not give this Gary person the satisfaction of knowing he scared her, that terror stormed through every cell.

"Gary Taub." The harsh tone ripped out of Connor.

"What are you doing here?" Ed asked as he took a step forward.

"Nuh-uh." Gary made a tsk-tsking sound. "Everyone stays where they are. Guns on the floor or the NCIS hero gets a bullet through his brain."

"No." She jumped forward and only Connor and Ben putting out their arms to stop her kept her from running into the madman's hands.

Gary laughed as he talked over her, acting as if her anguish bored him. "Although, I'm not sure how devastating Ben's murder would be to anyone. His own father is disgusted and embarrassed by him, isn't he, Ben?"

"Ask him." Ben said the words through a locked jaw as his intense gaze drilled into Jocelyn.

She knew he wanted her to stand still. To not antagonize the lunatic with the gun. Despite the fear pumping through her, she had no intention of starting a battle that ended with bodies scattered all over the floor. But if Gary went for Ben, her control would never hold.

Connor stiffened his stance but his gun's barrel never left the direct line to Gary's head. "That's enough."

"Touching." Gary spoke right into Ben's ear.

"Looks like I'm wrong. A woman who barely knows you thinks you're worth saving. Maybe if she'd spent more time with you she'd know you're not worth it."

What was that…? Jocelyn blinked. She swore Connor and Joel closed in on Gary but she hadn't seen them move and they hadn't made a noise. She chalked it up to an optical illusion, maybe wishful thinking. With a second glance at the floor, she knew the sensation of shrinking space wasn't in her head. Connor's foot had inched in.

She glanced up for verification. Connor didn't look at her but his head dipped in what she took for a nod.

"Let's show her how wrong she is about you." Gary pushed on Ben's shoulder. "Get on your knees."

"Not happening."

"I said no moving." Gary's voice kicked up as he scanned the room. "You have one second to get those guns on the ground or Mr. NCIS will have a nasty accident."

"We're listening." The anger left Connor's voice. He sounded reasonable and calm, as if he wanted to have a nice chat over coffee. "You clearly want to tell us something. Do it."

"I'm afraid I don't have time."

"He's transferring money." Kent said the words so fast they ran into one long word.

Gary barked right back. "Shut up."

"He's running out of time." Kent swallowed and shifted his weight until he balanced his palms against his desk. "He has less than an hour."

"Now is not the time to play the hero, Kent. You know what will happen if you do. I believe I've made that clear over the last few days."

The pieces clicked right into place. Jocelyn saw the total picture. Kent being blackmailed. His wife in danger. "You have his wife hidden somewhere. You're threatening her to get Kent to help you."

Gary's grin bordered on feral. "Aren't you the smart one?"

"Is she even still alive?" It hurt Jocelyn to ask the question.

The idea of this woman, and Pamela, being dead at this man's hands made Jocelyn's stomach heave. An overwhelming wave of sadness crashed over her as the very real possibility that the men she'd come to believe in so much might be too late this time.

The horrible thought floated through her mind and she used all of her concentration to push it away. The worry and the guilt. Later, in the quiet with no one around, she'd analyze everything and let her emotions bubble over. Right now she needed Gary's attention on her while Connor and Joel, and possibly Ben, followed through with whatever plan had them shrinking the room by barely moving their feet.

"Sharon is dead?" Ed asked.

Kent lost all restraint. He came around the side of the desk with his arms waving and eyes wide with fear. "No!"

Jocelyn shifted along the front of the desk or else Kent would have run right into her. He seemed blind to anything but getting to the man holding his wife.

"So, all this really comes down to a burglary." Ben almost shouted the comment. The force of his voice stopped Kent's drive to Gary. "Just greed."

He rolled his eyes. "Don't be stupid. I have plenty of money."

It had been so long since Jocelyn hated someone. When she'd changed her life and her name, she'd promised not to wallow in negative emotions. She had too many other issues to handle.

But with Gary it didn't fester. It imploded, fueling the white-hot heat rolling over her. "Then what? You like kidnapping women and faking bank robberies?"

"Some men might find your feistiness refreshing, Ms. Raine. I am not one of them." Gary's dark eyes squinted at her. "You may wish to keep that in mind."

"What's the plan here?" Connor asked, dragging the attention back to him.

"You're going to spend some time in the bank vault while Kent unlocks the door to his other office upstairs. The one filled with computers and servers and, not too long from now, the information I seek." Gary nodded to his sidekick. "Colin here will watch over all of you while Kent and I take care of our pressing business."

"What does that mean?" But she knew. There was no way this Gary guy would leave witnesses. He ran a legitimate business. Had clients. He couldn't afford to have anyone out there knowing the kind of man he really was.

"Kent looks like a loser, doesn't he?" Gary laughed while he said it, as if he was telling some sort of private joke. "You'd never know the government trusts him and this small know-nothing bank to transfer huge sums of money to undercover field operatives. The money comes in and Kent's other division, the one he can't discuss without risking the government's wrath, holds the money, then transfers it into the appropriate accounts."

Connor's gaze narrowed even further. "So, this *is* about money."

So much death because one stupid man had to collect more and own more. She hated men like him. Had spent the last year outrunning the memory of one. "You're a petty thief. No better than the guys who rob gas stations."

"Jocelyn." Ben gave the warning. One word, her name, and a look of boiling fury.

Gary gave the clock behind Kent a quick glance. "You may want to listen to your boyfriend and stop talking."

"But she has a point," Connor said.

The sound coming from Gary sounded like a growl. "Money is the least of my concerns. This is about information."

Joel switched his gun to aim at Colin. "Enlighten us."

"Why not? You won't be able to use what you learn to your benefit anyway." Gary smirked, clearly pleased to share his brilliance. "For that moment when the money goes in, identifying account information for those top secret accounts is not as well protected as it normally is. Parts are decoded and, with the right equipment, which I have, can be caught in that fraction of a second before shutting off again."

Any way she added it up, the answer was money. The man who professed to have enough wanted more. "And you take all the cash."

"No, I'm grabbing the account information. The whereabouts of the people in the program. There are people who would pay for it. Or I can make the necessary arrangements to have an undercover operative found. My choice. Their lives will be in my hands."

"This is about your brother," Joel said.

"Murdered." Gary uttered the horrible word but didn't say anything else.

"You're saying this is about revenge for you?" Ed asked.

Tension choked the room. Jocelyn wanted the team to move. They were waiting and talking, and it didn't make sense.

Gary's eyes turned wild as he spoke. "My brother's team failed to protect him and he got killed. I got a bogus story about his death. Facts I knew were wrong."

Connor nodded. "But he worked undercover and no one could talk."

"But they could pay, and they're going to. They let him die. Hell, they may have killed him to shut him up. Doesn't matter. I'll burn it all down."

"Which means we all need to die, as well." Her terror cut off her breath and threatened to suffocate her.

Greed was simple and straightforward. A ridiculous excuse for so much pain, but an emotion she saw at the hospital in the way heirs fought over dying parents and insurance companies battled about paying out claims. But vengeance came from a twisted place. It consumed, burning everything in its path. Worse, it meant Gary wouldn't care how many people he took with him so long as he went out in his brother's name.

"How do you expect to take us all on?" Connor asked.

"I have the gun and your man." Gary pressed the gun against Ben's head again. "And I'm not alone."

Joel laughed. "Colin here? I'm pretty sure when the bullets start flying he'll run away like the scared animal he is."

"I think I could take him," Jocelyn said, because at this point she might be able to strangle them all with her bare hands.

"You are welcome to try, Ms. Raine."

Kent leaned harder against the desk, and the legs groaned under the impact of his full weight. "He has a partner."

"Oh, yes." Gary shot her one of those smiles that promised pain. "Did I fail to mention that?"

"I think we've heard enough." Ben looked to Connor.

He nodded. "Yep."

The last thing she saw was Ben diving for her. His arms wrapped around her, and his big body slammed into hers. The momentum sent them flying into the desk, then crashing to the hard floor. The room blurred around them as she struggled to bring it all into focus.

Ed reached for Kent, and Connor took Gary out

with one bullet to the forehead. While she rolled over the floor tucked against Ben's chest, shots rang out and men yelled. A loud thud echoed in her ears as Gary fell in a boneless whoosh.

Then silence.

Struggling to sit up and settling for balancing on her elbows with Ben still covering her, she glanced over his arm and into the chaos. Connor and Joel grabbed Colin's guns and shoved him hard against the wall.

"You okay?" Desperation pounded off Ben.

She looked up at him while her hands roamed over his arms and she scanned his chest for blood. "You?"

"Answer me. Are you—"

"Fine." She cupped a hand over his cheek. "Thanks to you."

Ben exhaled. "We wanted him to talk. Tell us as much of his scheme as we could before mobilizing the takedown."

Her head jerked back. "The big stall and all that talk was some tactic?"

"Yeah. We run it in a drill a thousand times per month. We know the signals and can do them without a word or movement. It's all in the eyes." Ben winked as he separated from her and reached out to Gary's body. Took out the other man's phone and pocketed his weapons.

Death had overtaken him during the fall. The

man's eyes were open and his arms spread out wide as blood ran from the wound in his head.

She doubted Connor missed shots much but he sure didn't miss from that distance.

"No!" Kent pushed out of Ed's grip and scrambled around the desk. "What did you do? My wife. I need to find Sharon."

Joel caught the other man before he ran right up Connor's back. "Colin here is going to help us with that."

"I don't know anything." Colin looked around. His body shook and his dark eyes were alive with fear. "Please."

Joel shook his head. "Oh, Colin. Begging?"

Between the frantic headshaking and grabbing at Connor's hand where it shoved against Colin's chest and held him to the wall, Jocelyn worried Colin might lose it right there. Worse, he'd shut down before they could get to Kent's wife.

Colin struggled and his body rocked. "Gary's partner kidnapped her, not me."

"Who's his partner?" Ed had moved up and joined in the semicircle penning Colin in.

"I don't know. Gary wouldn't tell me. Said the partner insisted on anonymity but had set the whole thing up."

With a hand extended down to her, Ben got to his feet, then pulled her up beside him. Then he was off. He broke right into the middle of the group of men and put his face close to Colin's. "Not believable."

"I swear. I don't know anything."

Joel whistled. "I hope for your sake that's not true."

Jocelyn joined in because despite all the rage whipping around and the poor woman hidden somewhere, she could not let these men kill an unarmed man. Honest and decent men, she couldn't imagine it happening, but the nerves in the room hovered at the breaking point. "The only reason to let you live is to find Sharon."

Colin's head thrashed against the wall. "I followed orders and hired the men who…" He broke off when he focused on her.

Maybe she could let them hurt Colin after all. "Tried to grab me."

"Did you, Colin? Was that your bright idea?" Ben's voice went deadly soft.

"Gary was obsessed with that note and the conversation Pamela overheard after hours." Those beady eyes focused on Jocelyn. "And you were right there behind him in the cashier line when Pamela recognized him."

"I'm thinking we're missing pieces here," Joel said.

At first Jocelyn couldn't figure out what the comment meant. She tried to remember every minute of that day. The actions mirrored every other time she went to the bank. Picking the right door, walking up. The deposit slip. Waiting in line...behind Gary.

The memory blindsided her. She opened her mouth, gasping for breath. She would have grabbed on to Ben but Kent started screaming.

"Where is Sharon?" With a strength that didn't match his size, Kent elbowed in between Connor and Ben.

"I don't know."

Joel sighed. "I wouldn't say that again."

"Enough." Ben put the gun to Colin's temple as he crowded in close with his arm pressed against Colin's throat.

Dizziness gripped her. "Ben, are you sure you—"

"You've heard about my reputation. You know I won't think twice about taking down another man, and today is your day. I'm going to pull this trigger. If a bullet doesn't come out, I will pull again." Ben followed through and aimed the weapon. "And no one here is going to stop me."

"You don't understand." Panic threaded through Colin's voice as he coughed and gagged against the force of Ben's heavy arm.

"In five...four..." Ben's monotone voice sounded like a clock.

"Stop him." Colin punched at Ben's arm and

the death grip crumpling his windpipe and holding him still.

Ben didn't flinch. Didn't move.

"I'm fine with this," Connor said.

"Me, too." Joel glanced over his shoulder.
"Ed?"

"Three...two..."

Ed nodded. "I'm good."

"A warehouse three..." Colin's words raced
together as his body shook from a coughing fit.
"Three exits down. Gary said one of his guys
would take care of her."

Ben eased back. "There."

"See, was that so hard?" Joel asked.

Kent blew out long breaths as he teetered on
the edge of hyperventilating. "We need to call
the police."

Connor raised an eyebrow as he looked at Ben.
"Which raises the Willoughby issue."

Something silent and profound passed between
Ben and Connor. She guessed it had something to
do with Colin's "take care of her" comment and
the worry Sharon was already gone.

It took a few seconds, but Ben finally spoke
up. "Let's get to Sharon first. Then we can figure out the partner situation."

Jocelyn knew then they suspected Willoughby.
A plant right in the police department. Again. She

wanted her experience to be the aberration. Now she feared it was the rule.

Kent's hands shook as he scooped his keys off the edge of his desk. "I can drive—"

Ben was already talking before the man got the sentence out. "You stay here. Jocelyn can wait with you. One of our teammates, Davis, is on the way to help out and see if there is any other information to retrieve here."

She had no idea when the call went out to the rest of the Corcoran team, but she wasn't surprised. Those watches they wore did everything. Could be Davis and Pax overheard the whole thing.

But one thing she did know. She wasn't staying behind. She was about to make that clear but Kent beat her to it.

"I'm coming with you." Kent stood up straight and his teeth had stopped chattering.

Jocelyn almost didn't recognize the strong man now compared to the sweating mess from a few minutes before. Nervous energy wafted around him. He still shifted and looked half-ready to leap across the room and take his chances running out the door, but there was a new determination coursing through him.

"No."

Jocelyn thought she knew what caused the change in Kent. "Ben, it's his wife."

She expected a fight. Maybe even a question about why that fact mattered. After all, he was single and used to going it alone.

Instead, he nodded. "Let's go."

Chapter Fifteen

They all raced to the warehouse. A nondescript, one-story building the length of a football field. From the outside it looked like something you might find on a farm. Breaking the lock on the entry door proved easy. Ben slammed the butt of his gun into it twice before Connor stepped in and shot the lock the rest of the way off.

Now they roamed through a series of slim hallways and tiny rooms. Ben had no idea what the space was used for, storage maybe, since boxes were piled everywhere, but the setup made them vulnerable as they maneuvered through the space two by two.

He walked next to Jocelyn gun up and eyes scanning, with Joel in front of her and Ed at her back. Ben didn't like the setup but no way was he leaving her outside to get nabbed by Gary's partner, whoever that might be.

In unison, they cleared section by section with Connor and Joel sneaking around each corner and checking the rooms first. Wires hung exposed from the cracked and missing ceiling tiles above them and papers scattered all over the floor.

They walked carefully and deliberately, making as little sound as possible. Even Kent, who was all but whimpering at this point, reduced most of his anxiety to shaking shoulders and chewing on his thumb.

Not that Ben could blame the guy. The idea of Jocelyn getting grabbed sliced right through him, splitting him in half. He'd seen Gary reaching for her back at the bank and had thrown a body block. He'd sacrificed his own body and he'd do it again if necessary. Anything to get her out of there safe and fast.

They came to a T in the hallways. Connor looked both ways, then grabbed Colin by the shirt collar. With his hands zip-tied behind his back, the guy couldn't do anything but struggle and spit. Connor shook him hard enough to stop even that. "Give us an idea."

Colin stuttered, "I've never been here."

Connor pushed his gun into Colin's back to let him know his patience had expired. "Wrong answer."

Kent shifted and sighed. "Please, we have to hurry."

"He's right." With a hand on Ben's forearm,

Jocelyn lowered her voice to a bare whisper. "Sharon could be running out of air."

Ben nodded. "Colin, I won't think twice about shooting you in the leg, then dragging you through the rest of the building."

"And I won't help you until we find her," Jocelyn said.

Ben knew it was an empty boast. She saved. It was pure instinct for her. He got it because the same drive to fix things beat wildly within him.

But he did love this fierce side of her. He'd watched her race here and there at the hospital, taking care and handling the blood and guts that spilled around her. This, the survival instinct, the way she fought off her doubts and fears and rose to every challenge, filled him with admiration and had his attraction to her zipping off the charts.

He was falling for this woman, and if they somehow survived the next few minutes, he'd tell her.

"Furnace room." Colin blew out a few long breaths, as if trying not to pass out. "He mentioned something about the furnace room."

Connor glanced past Colin. "Joel, do your thing."

"What are you doing?" Kent clawed at Joel's hands as he flipped out a phone and his fingers danced across the screen. "We can't stop."

Joel didn't look up. "Construction blueprints filed with the city."

"What?" Ed asked as he pulled Kent back and pushed him against the nearest wall.

Joel started walking. "This way."

They moved, faster now, rounding two corners and ducking. Watching each step as they hit a wider hallway where the ceiling had been ripped out and wires snaked the walls and floor. They got to a door without markings and Ben stepped up. He tested the knob and found it unlocked. The whole thing smelled like a trap.

"Careful," Connor said as he nodded.

Ben flipped the knob and the door slammed open. He went in high and Connor took low, with Joel watching their backs.

Nothing.

The room was empty. There wasn't so much as a crate or a box inside. Ben didn't know what it meant. This room was clean for some reason, the only one in the place without stuff strewn all over the floor, and that was enough to convince Ben not to go one step farther. "Back out, following the same steps."

Connor nodded. "Got it."

A minute later they all crowded at what looked like a hallway to nowhere. Jocelyn had Joel's phone and was staring at something.

"It's back here." She made the announcement

and grabbed for the shelves at the end of the hall. "This has to be fake."

Ed shook his head. "There's nothing there."

Wide-eyed and half-desperate, she shot Ben a pleading look. "Help me."

Joel looked at his phone, then nodded. "Nice job."

Holstering their weapons, the two joined her while Connor kept watch. They slid their hands over the dusty shelves and kicked away the piles of wood and electrical supplies on the floor that blocked a better grip.

It took less than a minute for them to tug and strain before the wood near Joel gave. The shelves moved out to reveal stacks of boxes behind. They all reached at the same time. Grunting and shuffling, they set up a line and unloaded.

Connor shoved Colin toward the front of the work area and took Ed's gun. "You don't need to guard him. There's nowhere for him to go."

Ben wiped the sweat off his forehead. The stagnant air of the windowless space had them all wheezing. Jocelyn's body shook from the force of her coughs, but she waved him off when he tried to get her to sit down.

Truth was Ben wanted all their help. There was a woman in there who could be dying. He'd had enough dying on his watch. This needed to be a win. For Kent, for Jocelyn, for all of them.

They got to the metal door and Joel went to work on the lock.

"Please hurry," Kent said from right over Joel's shoulder.

The pick didn't work and the bullets ricocheted, promising more damage. Connor stepped in. He ripped the top pocket of his vest open and took out a small packet.

Explosives. Ben pushed the crowd back into the hallway as Connor dropped to one knee and put the putty on the door. "We need to take cover."

"No, you can't." Kent tried to go up and over Ben. "She could be right on the other side."

Ben caught the older man around the chest and shoved him back. "It's the only way in."

The comment was a lie. There were other ways. Longer ways. Plans that would guarantee his wife ran out of air. This was the best choice.

Ben didn't say any of that. He was too busy rushing Jocelyn around the corner. They hunkered down and he dropped his body over hers, trying to cover every inch. She protected her head and he protected the rest of her. He glanced up only to see Joel running over to join them.

"Heads down and stick to the wall," Joel said before nodding to Connor. "You're good."

The words were out and the deafening bang had sparks flying and chunks of metal and plaster falling around them. Pebbles of whatever was left rained down on them and littered the ground.

Ben glanced up and saw the door hanging on its hinges with half of it blown away. The hole led to the dark room beyond. When he started to stand up, Jocelyn tugged on his arm.

"I am not staying out here, so don't ask." Her eyes flashed with fire and her stern expression suggested no one mess with her.

Not that he intended to. This wasn't an argument he intended to have. "Since there's a partner hanging around somewhere, as soon as we break in and secure the place, I want you right next to me."

They stood up and she brushed the thin film of dust off her face. "Romantic."

They made a rush to the door, with Kent itching to go in first. Connor's voice stopped him. "We don't know what we're going to see in here."

"I'm a nurse." Jocelyn pushed to the front and waited for Joel to clear the electrical wires and chunks of metal in their way.

"No offense but there are things that can happen and—"

Jocelyn sighed at Connor. "She might need medical attention and I plan on giving it to her no matter what you say."

Fighting was the wrong tact. This needed to happen. "She's going," Ben said.

Joel shoved the last of the debris out of the way and nodded toward the inside. "We're in."

"Hold Kent," Connor ordered.

"But I want—"

Ed slapped a hand on Kent before he could run. "Got him."

Ben and Connor slipped in, checking each corner and the cabinet on the far side.

Connor opened the door and felt around. "Clear."

Ben nodded. "Clear."

Jocelyn rushed in, then came to a hard stop. "That's a—"

"Box on a table." Looked like a coffin. Ben tried to keep his voice steady but rage made it vibrate.

Someone on Gary's payroll put a living, breathing woman in a box. Cut off her air and waited for her to die. What kind of sick bastard did that?

"Get it open. Now," Ben ordered.

"No, no, no." Kent's wail bounced off every wall. It was a high, keening cry like something a wounded animal might make.

The sound was so desperate and raw, Ben wanted to cover his ears. At least grab Jocelyn and run her out of there. Anything not to watch that level of intense human pain.

Kent tripped over something in his walk across the room and would have fallen if Connor didn't catch him. "Okay, settle down. I need you to stand here."

Ed stepped up and let Kent lean on him. "I got him."

He shook his head as the tears ran down his face. The pain was so obvious, so palpable, Ben couldn't even watch him. His gaze went to Jocelyn's pale face, and the terror mirrored Kent's.

Ben was ready to do the one thing he could do. Rip the damn box apart with his hands if necessary. "I have to get to her."

Joel joined him and they grunted and shoved. They tore the top of the box off, ignoring the nails and the bites of wood and stabs against their hands. The wood creaked and snapped. After a few yanks they had the top completely off.

The scene inside didn't give Ben one ounce of comfort. A woman, blonde and still, wearing a shirt and pants lay there unmoving. Ben guessed the shirt had once been white. Now blood stained it a dull red.

Joel shook his head as he stepped back, as if he couldn't look one more minute.

"Is she breathing?" Jocelyn shoved her way to the front and put a hand to the still woman's throat. "I've got a weak pulse and blood."

Kent had his fingers wrapped around the side of the box as he stared down at his wife. "Take her out."

"No, leave her there. There could be broken bones." Jocelyn pushed all the hands away and went to work. She listened to her heart and shifted her clothing. "Let me check her."

Connor tried to move Kent away from the box. "Why don't we—"

"You are not going to stop me from checking on my wife." Kent turned on him, throwing out his arms and ready for battle until Connor nodded.

"Is she alive?" Ed asked as he peeked around Joel.

A beeping started somewhere near Jocelyn. She spun around with her arms up and Ben aimed his gun. He just didn't know what was attacking this time.

"Ease up. She has my phone." Joel reached over and slid it out of Jocelyn's back pocket. A couple of clicks and he looked up, his mouth even more grim than before. "We've got company."

"What?" Jocelyn's eyes narrowed. "Who?"

"Willoughby, I bet." That man showed up at the wrong places at the exact wrong times. Ben didn't trust him and certainly didn't want him sneaking in from behind.

"Being here will get you in trouble," Ed said. "That detective might fire first. Go meet him and I'll stay with Kent and Sharon."

No way was Ben agreeing to that. "We're not afraid of Willoughby."

"But she can identify her attacker, which means it might not be safe for her to see the detective." Ed glanced at Kent, then back to the team. "If she wakes up."

"You think the police detective is the partner?" Kent shook his head. "That doesn't make sense with what Gary said about his partner."

"Meaning?" Connor asked.

"He talked about resources in the police department but made them sound low on the food chain. Not his partner."

A loud intake of breath cut off whatever came next. Ben heard whimpering and saw Jocelyn lean over the box. She whispered something as she tried to hold down the arms flailing around her. The woman kicked and slapped as the high-pitched screams, shrill and terrified, filled the room.

Ben looked to Connor and Joel. They both frowned as the horrifying sound wound up and got louder.

"It's okay. You're safe." Jocelyn kept up the soothing words as she held the men back with a stiff shake of her head. "Take deep breaths."

Kent stood still as if frozen in place as soon as the pained screams started. "Sharon."

The yelling subsided, decreasing to sobbing. She hiccuped and sniffed. "Kent?"

"You can move your hands and feet." Jocelyn nodded to Ben and he came in closer. "He's going to help you up. Kent's here, too."

Under Jocelyn's direction, Ben put a hand under Sharon's shoulders as Kent held her hand and Jocelyn checked her back. "Let's get you—"

The frail woman's body heaved and another scream tore out of her. She was crying and pointing. She grabbed on to Jocelyn and hid behind her.

Ben glanced over, thinking he'd see Willoughby standing there. "What the—"

Colin and Ed both stood blocking the door. Ben remembered Connor taking Ed's gun but he held a weapon. Colin's restraints were gone. On closer look, they'd both found guns, which meant they had more than the ones they showed they were carrying before.

"She wasn't supposed to wake up," Ed said.

Joel shifted position, coming out from behind Connor and slipping his phone back into his pocket. "Guess we know the identity of Gary's partner."

"To be fair, Colin didn't know until now, but he's loyal." Ed shrugged. "Which is smart because I plan to be the winning side here. I've been working on this for too long. There's too much money at stake."

"And Sharon can identify you," Connor said.

Ed smiled. "Sorry, boys."

He swung his arm around in an arc as he fired. Bullets pinged and chunks of plaster exploded from the wall. While firing, they all ducked and dived for what little cover the room provided. In the small space, something was bound to hit someone. Ben planned for it to be the bad guys.

Ed ran for the doorway but Ben's bullet caught him in the back. Another from either Joel or Connor brought him down in a dead sprawl. Colin had a longer job getting to safety. With Ed gone, Colin's shield disappeared but he kept firing even as he yelled.

The booming sounds came from every direction. Ben tried to pivot around the box as he shot. He had to get Jocelyn to safety. She'd thrown her upper body over Sharon and for a second Ben thought she'd been hit.

He reached her right as he felt a burning across his neck. That fast his vision blurred. His grip failed him right as his legs gave out. With one last lunge, he snagged Jocelyn's arm and brought her to the floor. She fought him but he rolled her under the table, giving her the best protection in the room.

He scrambled away, trying to draw attention

to himself. Shifting, he put his knees under him, thinking to get up and catch Colin before he snuck away, but the room flipped on him. The last image he had was of a shadow looming in the doorway.

Then his head hit the floor.

JOCELYN DUCKED UNDER the table. She wasn't quite sure how she got there. Pieces of memories ran through her mind. Ben grabbed her. Sharon… poor Sharon. Even now Jocelyn could hear her shouting and begging to get out of the box.

Jocelyn peeked up through her arms and saw Colin make a final desperate run for the doorway as a bullet hit his thigh and Connor yelled at him to stop. Blood ran and a burning smell filled the room. Jocelyn blinked and saw boots. Her gaze traveled up until she reached Willoughby's face. He stood there in full riot gear. When Colin made a final lunge, Willoughby cracked him in the head with the end of his gun.

He glanced around at the wreckage. Blood and broken supplies everywhere. "Someone going to tell me what's going on?"

Connor stepped up carefully. One foot at a time, gun still raised. "How did you get here in time?"

"Was watching at the bank and followed you here." Willoughby nodded in Joel's direction.

"Then I got a call from him and all I could hear was someone talking about money and the shooting started. We were a few hallways away and I followed the noises to here."

"This is the one time it's good someone else drove, since being followed helped," Joel said as his shoulders eased and he abandoned battle mode.

"Okay." Connor blew out a long breath. "Good thinking, Joel."

Willoughby motioned behind him. "Got my men with me."

Jocelyn watched the police officers file in behind Willoughby in the doorway. He'd brought everyone. He rushed in to help and she didn't know what to make of that. At some point she'd have to apologize for assuming he was with Gary. It was an old reflex tied to the uniform.

"He's the one?" Willoughby used the toe of his boot to nudge Ed's unmoving arm.

Connor nodded. "Him and Gary Taub, who's back at the bank. Dead."

"A few of my men are there." Willoughby waved his men in. "Secure this scene, too. Everyone you see moving in here is clear."

Jocelyn struggled to her feet, still unable to believe Willoughby, the jerk who threw his weight around, had ridden in at the last minute to contain the situation. She looked at Sharon, who nodded and mouthed that she was okay.

Jocelyn didn't agree. "Sharon needs an ambulance."

"Please help her," Kent said.

Jocelyn noticed the blood on Connor's face from what looked like a nick across his cheek and the shot to Kent's wrist. He held it but didn't complain. In the end the desk jockey had turned out to be quite the savior for his wife.

She turned around to smile at her own savior. "Ben, are you—"

Connor was already moving. He dropped to his knees at the far end of the box, right in the corner. "Ben's down. We need an ambulance."

It was as if someone flicked a switch. Police officers came into the room. Willoughby got on his radio as sirens rang out in the distance.

Her mind went blank. Sounds were muffled and everyone seemed to move in slow motion. She saw Joel's mouth as he cried out and slid in next to Ben. But the walls closed in on her. She stared at Ben's still body and the blood covering Connor's hand as he pressed it against Ben's neck.

"No, no…no…" She didn't know she'd said the words until she pushed Joel out of the way and shoved in next to Ben. He was so still, his skin almost gray.

The room whirled to life again.

She was not losing him. Not now that she'd found him and had fallen so hard and so deeply that she couldn't figure out how to separate herself from him.

Without thinking, she whipped her shirt off, leaving only a thin tank top on. She rolled the material into a ball and pressed it against Ben's neck. Blood soaked the material and covered her hand. Still, she pushed and ground, using all her strength to stanch the flow of blood.

Dipping down, she listened for breathing, tried to watch his chest rise. Nothing happened and her frantic search for a pulse turned up only the weakest flicker. "You will not die on me."

She wanted everything with this man. She would not watch the life seep out of him.

One of his eyes opened. A haze covered it and she doubted he could even see her. She grabbed for his hand with her free one. "I'm here, Ben."

"I'm sorry."

"Don't talk."

"It meant everything that you trusted me." His head lulled to the side. "I'm sorry it ended like this."

His eyes rolled back into his head and panic tore at her insides.

"I hate your job. I refuse to deal with the danger and fear." The words flowed out of her. She barely knew what she was saying. She just knew the fear infected her like a poison and she wanted it out. "No more, Ben. Do you hear me?"

But he couldn't. He was unconscious and deathly still. Seeing him like that filled her with a fury that kicked around her insides and had her doubling over in pain. Her muscles shook as she fought to hold him steady. She couldn't tip his head back for CPR, so she put her fingers against his jaw and lowered it.

The position wasn't perfect but she didn't have a choice. "Joel, hold this tight against his throat and do not let go for any reason."

Joel nodded as they shifted positions.

Connor shouted in the background to the people slipping in and out of the room. "We need an ambulance now. Get it here."

Willoughby helped Kent sit down and lifted Sharon out of the box. The chaos raged on but Jocelyn's focus stayed on the CPR count and watching Ben's chest for any signs of life. Her arms ached and her heart hammered hard enough for her to feel it in every limb.

"Jocelyn, he's not—"

She didn't even spare Joel a glance. "He will live. I will not walk away until I know he's okay."

And he had to be okay.

Chapter Sixteen

Ben heard shouting in his head. Male voices, then Jocelyn's. They screamed at him as a rush of what sounded like water beat against the inside of his brain. He wanted to fight against it. Find quiet. But Jocelyn... He ran toward her.

His eyes popped open and confusion settled in. Lights came into focus above him and he could make out the tiny dots in the ceiling tiles. He heard the beep of machines and smelled the antiseptic. He tried to move his head but something held his neck still, and even that small twitch had pain thundering against his skull.

He took it all in. Every piece, including the pale blue walls and the railings on the bed. He was in a hospital.

His eyes finally focused and instead of seeing the woman he wanted, he saw blond hair and scruff. Davis.

"Where's Jocelyn?" Ben ground his back teeth together and lifted a shoulder off the mattress.

"Hold on there." Davis held a hand against Ben's chest. "She's fine."

"She and Joel went to bug your doctors." Connor's head appeared above Ben. "Apparently she's not happy with how long it's taking you to wake up."

"You staying there or do I have to punch you to keep you down?" When Ben gave a small nod, Davis sat in the chair next to the bed. "You look terrible, by the way."

"I can always count on you for reassuring words." Ben tried to laugh but something in his neck pulled and yanked, sending a headache spinning through his brain. He lifted his hand and felt a thick bandage. He remembered the burning sensation. "Did I get shot in the neck?"

Davis nodded. "Yep. Kind of lame. You're supposed to duck."

"This from the job when you were too busy hiding in your house to help." Seeing Davis's mouth flatten, Ben felt a pang of guilt the second he made the joke.

"Not by choice."

"I wanted Lara safe," Connor said.

Davis shook his head. "For the record, I'm not riding a desk for the next seven months."

"Understood."

Ben wanted to run a hand over his face. That battled with his need to shut his eyes. He'd get to that as soon as he laid eyes on Jocelyn. He just had to see for himself she was fine. The idea of her hunting down doctors eased some of the anxiety knocking around inside him, but a guy had to check these things out for himself.

"Women," he said under his breath, knowing this group would understand the sentiment.

"You got problems with one?" Connor asked with amusement in his voice.

The memories tore into him. He went from blank to having a full-motion picture of the gunfire in his head. She stood in the middle of the shooting, protecting Sharon. Threw her body over Sharon and ignored her own safety.

Jocelyn had begged him not to die, then cursed him and his job. Every horrible second spooled out in front of him and he felt helpless to calm it all down.

"This was too close." He whispered it more in his head, not realizing he'd said it out loud until Connor agreed.

"But she did great. Kept you alive long enough to get you help. We owe her."

No, they didn't understand. They were praising her. Even now, Connor told Davis stories about all she'd done and how she stood up to him.

Ben listened but the same warning kept flashing in his mind. He broke into the cheering session. "She shouldn't have had to do any of it."

Connor frowned. "Gary was after her. You were the bodyguard."

"And next time I'll bring the danger to her door. And the time after that." The fear. That was what he remembered the most. Her dropped mouth and pale lips. The panic that had her eyes darting as yet another man leveled a gun at her head. "Tell me I'm wrong."

The hollowed-out feeling in his stomach wouldn't go away. Jocelyn in danger qualified as the one thing he could not handle. Gunfire, chases, his blowhard father, the wrath that went along with dismantling the NCIS...those were rough circumstances, but livable. Seeing someone put Jocelyn in a box... He closed his eyes as his mind rebelled and his stomach churned at the idea.

"It doesn't have to be like that," Connor said in a low voice.

"Where's your wife? Jana, why isn't she here?" Ben winced but he had to ask.

Connor's face went blank, as if all the life leached out of it. "Visiting her—"

"We all know that's not true. Something happened. Likely something about the intense work we do drove you guys apart."

Connor wrapped his hands around the bed railings tight enough for his knuckles to turn white.

"Maybe you should stop talking like you know about my personal life."

"That's enough," Davis said.

"Tell me I'm wrong, Connor." When Davis tried to talk again, Ben turned on him, too. "And you're twisted up trying to protect your pregnant wife. You both know what I'm talking about."

Davis put a palm flat against the top of Ben's pillow, and the mattress dipped. "But she is my wife. We worked through the danger stuff and we're together."

"It's so much." Waves of exhaustion pummeled Ben. "The stuff with the NCIS isn't dying down. My father won't even speak to me. How do I bring a woman into that? How do I ask a woman who has known violence and survived it to wade back into it with me?"

"She is not weak." Connor punctuated each word.

She was anything but. Ben had known that from the beginning. Her strength was part of the reason he was falling so hard, so fast. "I know that."

Davis answered, "Then give her a chance to see if she can handle your life. Don't push her away."

Ben couldn't move his head or block the pain out. "Right, do that and have our lives get more entwined and then, what, I pick her broken body up out of an alley?"

"Ben, come on." Davis pushed off from the bed and stood up straight again. "That's not going to happen."

"You can't promise that." Man, Ben wanted him to. He wanted a guarantee that Jocelyn would be okay. He wanted to know he'd never be the one to put her in a position where fear gripped her.

"I wouldn't be married and having a kid if I didn't believe it."

"I care about this woman. Really care." Those weren't words he said easily and they didn't even touch the full load of what he felt for Jocelyn. "Like, I don't even understand how I can be falling for her this hard."

Davis rolled his eyes. "Then let her in."

"How can I ask her to take a chance on me?"

THE MAN WAS LUCKY he was confined to a hospital bed or she might just march right over there and smack him. Jocelyn couldn't believe the nonsense he was spewing. Sweet on one level, but frustrating on every other. Did he actually think after everything they'd gone through, after he stuck by her when she was being hunted, that she would walk away?

Men.

"You should be asking me that question, not

them." She walked into the room, keeping her arms wrapped around her stomach.

She was so stupidly happy to see him awake and breathing that she wanted to crawl up there with him and throw her arms around him, but he had to get his head out of his butt first. If he planned to go all martyr on her, she would fight him every step of the way.

"I want you safe," he said, ignoring the friends standing on either side of him and watching only her.

"Which, in your mind, can only mean not being near you." Never mind that she wasn't in danger because of him. "Well, I would remind you that you're the one who did the chasing. You asked me out. I said no, and you kept coming back."

Davis smiled at that.

Between the colorless skin and drawn expression, Ben looked ten seconds away from passing out. "There are people who think being near me is a death wish. My track record isn't good."

Her heart broke a little for him. She cursed his stubborn father and everyone else who dumped their insecurities on Ben.

She used all her control to stand in that spot rather than go to him. "I don't see you that way. Not me. Not your team. No one in this room."

"What if you're all wrong?"

"So you live a celibate life from now on? How realistic is that." Now that they'd slept together, she knew there was no way. He didn't hold back in the bedroom. No way could he deny himself.

And he better not unleash all that passion on anyone but her.

He gave a quick glance at his friends but they didn't move. "I want you somewhere safe."

"Why don't you let me decide where I go and who I'm with?"

"Jocelyn, I'm—"

She leaned in with a hand behind her ear. "What, are you sorry?"

"Don't do this."

She ignored how his voice grew louder. "You better at least be sorry for the right thing."

Color flooded his cheeks. "Meaning what?"

Anger. Good, she could handle anger. Indifference would kill them.

All those fears of being on the wrong end of violence had held her back. With Ben, something inside her had broken free. That shield she clenched in front of her had crumbled. She needed his to do the same.

"Don't you get it, Ben? You should be sorry for nearly bleeding out in my arms and wasting your last bit of energy on giving me the 'it's been swell but we're over' speech." The memories zoomed through her, taking her voice louder with every word. "Who does that? What kind of man puts his girlfriend through that?"

Davis shook his head. "Oh, dude."

She pointed at him. "Exactly. Davis gets it."

"Girlfriend?" Ben tried to sit up straighter but the bandage limited his movements and the wound had him wincing.

Knowing he was in pain took the edge off her anger. Her frustration came both from seeing him rushed away in an ambulance and hearing him talk about walking away from her for good. She didn't want to deal with either ever again.

"Yes, Ben. I don't sleep around. I barely date."

"I know that."

She could only assume his stubbornness made him blind. "Then you know I risked everything on you."

His intense gaze didn't leave her face. "Because you were in danger."

"No, because I want to be with you, talk to you, sleep with you." Careful not to hit the bed, she stepped in when Connor moved back. She slid her thigh on the mattress next to his legs and stopped there even though she ached to get closer. "All of it and all the time."

He picked up her hand and played with her fingers. "All the violence."

"Goes with your job. I won't lie. That's not easy for me. It scares me to death." When he gave her a pained frown, she rushed to finish her point. "But I also get that you have friends and people who watch out for you and that you're careful. You don't take stupid risks."

Davis cleared his throat. "He's usually on his game, though he's not doing so well here."

"You begged for a date." She ignored Connor's laugh and Ben's scowl. "You were relentless and now you want out? No. I'm not giving you a choice. You wanted me? Well, now I want you back."

"You do?"

"I might even love you a little, which we're not going to talk about now, certainly not with company listening in, but the one thing I am not doing is leaving you." The truth sat out there now and she couldn't call it back. She didn't even want to. After everything they'd been through, he deserved to know the truth.

"I like her," Davis said.

Connor nodded. "She fits in with the other women in the group."

Davis made a sound like a hum. "And it wouldn't be bad to have a nurse on staff."

Ben didn't even spare them a glance. He kept his attention on her as he slipped his fingers through hers and held on tight. "Both of you get out."

"Maybe we're watching out for her," Connor said.

She didn't break eye contact either. Couldn't. "I can handle Ben on my own."

"Yeah, I think you can." Connor patted Ben on the shoulder. "We'll find Joel and Pax and come back later."

Davis laughed. "Much later."

Ben barely waited until the door closed behind his friends. "Love?"

She knew he'd grab on to that one word. Other men, no. They'd ignore it and try to work around it. Not Ben. She said *love,* and excitement flared in his eyes. "A little and it's just at the beginning stages, so don't kill it by being a moron."

He tugged her closer. "Come here."

"Oh, now you get bossy." She put her hands on either side of his shoulders. "I'll tolerate that, since you've been shot and stabbed and who knows what else. But as your nurse, I would suggest you be careful."

"I'm taking my bossiness cues from you." He tried to lift his head and hissed instead.

She took pity on him and leaned in closer, letting her lips skim over his. "Honestly, you could use a clue or two."

"I'm sorry," he said when they broke apart again.

"For?" And this was a test. If he didn't get it

right…well, she wasn't going anywhere. But she didn't want to fight with him, either. "And do not say putting me in danger or anything like that."

"How about for trying to push you away?"

She kissed him again. Short and sweet but enough for the desired connection. "Better."

"I want you safe and am willing to do whatever that takes." His hand brushed up and down her thigh. "But I'm also not stupid. When a woman like you throws around the *L* word, a man listens."

The words knocked down the rest of her protective wall. This man, this amazing man who carried a gun and could probably scale buildings if he wanted to, meant everything. "Are you sure?"

"That falling thing." He toyed with the end of her hair. "The love—"

She put her thumb and forefinger an inch apart. "Little bit and at the beginning."

He pushed those fingers farther apart. "Me, too."

Her heart jumped. "Really?"

"Why do you think I'm so desperate to lock you away where my job and this life can't touch you?"

"I lived for months and months being afraid." Talking about her life back then stole something from her, but she needed him to understand. "I'm not afraid of you."

"After what happened to you and how you had to fight…all the attacks over the last week…how is that possible?"

Hearing him rendered almost speechless was just about the most flattering, attractive thing ever. The idea she could knock this controlled man off his game made her smile. "I think it had something to do with seeing a policeman step up and do the right thing."

"Willoughby?"

She still had to figure out a way to apologize to the guy. He had even come to the hospital to check on Ben, Sharon and Kent and never once threatened or suggested the crimes rolled out any way other than the way they actually did. No blame. "He came through, but that wasn't all."

"Meaning?"

"Your team thrives on the challenge of the job without enjoying the violence. That makes a difference. You view danger as a necessary evil but don't seek it out, and that matters to me." The words spilled out of her. She needed him to know she didn't lump him in with the law-enforcement types she'd known before. "With you guys, danger and gunfire are normal, and I don't fully understand that, but I've seen you all handle it without turning into the scary people you hunt."

He lifted their joined hands and placed a kiss against her skin. "Thank you."

"Your dad is wrong, you know." Now, there was a man she wanted to shake.

Ben's eyes closed. When they opened again, they were heavy and a bit sad. "He's set in his ways."

"No, Ben. He's wrong. You're a hero." She balanced a hand against his pillow and leaned in real close. "My hero."

He skimmed his hand over her stiff arm. "Does that mean you'll come home with me?"

The question sent that tiny spark of hope inside her roaring to a flaring flame. He was talking about them. No more doom and gloom and mentions of leaving her behind.

She loved it. "You think you're leaving the hospital so soon?"

"I thought you'd sign me out and take care of me in our bed at home." His hand found her waist. "If that's okay with you."

Her heart danced with excitement. "Our?"

"You really want to go back to your apartment?"

He meant the attack in her family room, but the lifeline he offered went beyond that one terrible night. Whether he knew it or not, he was talking about building a future. "I need to be wherever you are."

"Then close that door and we'll start practicing in private." He tapped the mattress. "I bet the bed moves."

She laughed as her head fell forward and her cheek brushed his. "I think we're actually pretty good at 'it' already."

"True, but that's not what I meant." She felt his warm breath across her ear right before he nuzzled her there. The kisses on her neck came next. "I'm thinking we need to work on turning a little into a lot."

Which was exactly what she wanted. "That's what I want."

"Then let's get started."

* * * * *

ReaderService.com

Manage your account online!

- Review your order history
- Manage your payments
- Update your address

*We've designed
the Harlequin® Reader Service
website just for you.*

Enjoy all the features!

- Reader excerpts from any series
- Respond to mailings and
  special monthly offers
- Discover new series available to you
- Browse the Bonus Bucks catalog
- Share your feedback

Visit us at:
ReaderService.com